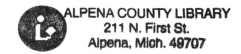

Caravan to America

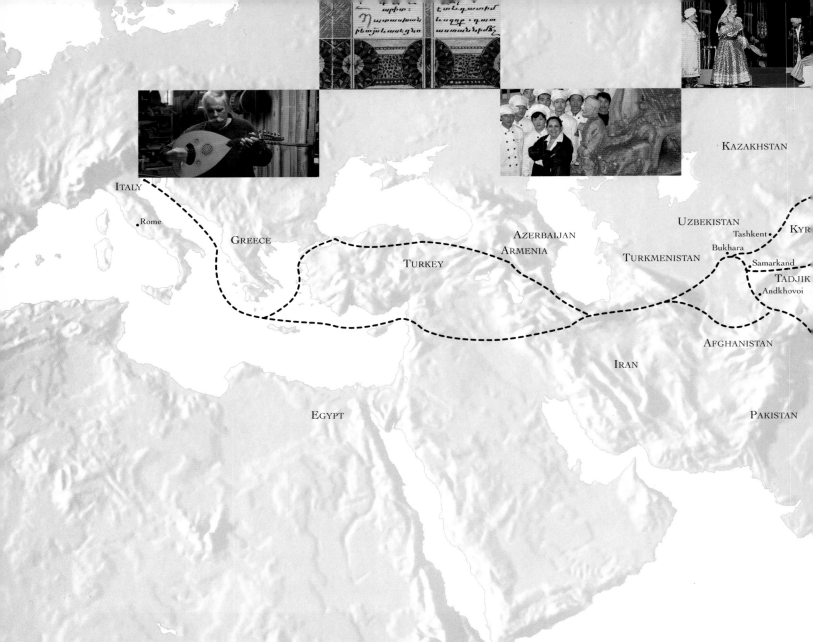

ITALY

Rome

GREECE

TURKEY

AZERBAIJAN
ARMENIA

EGYPT

IRAN

KAZAKHSTAN

UZBEKISTAN
Tashkent
KYR
Bukhara
Samarkand
TADJIK
Andkhovoi

TURKMENISTAN

AFGHANISTAN

PAKISTAN

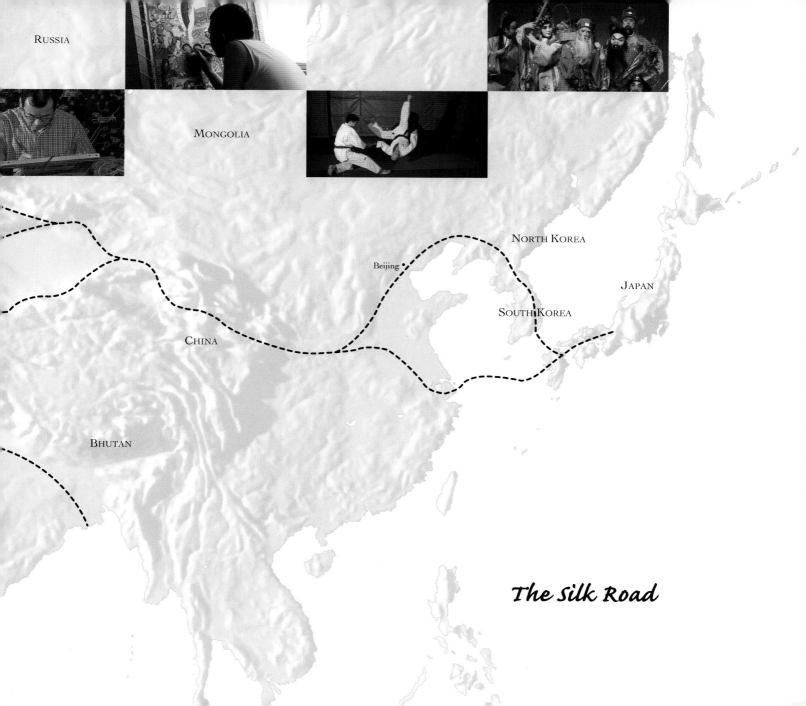

RUSSIA

MONGOLIA

NORTH KOREA

JAPAN

Beijing

SOUTH KOREA

CHINA

BHUTAN

The Silk Road

This eighth-century Chinese ceramic sculpture of Central
Asian musicians served as inspiration for the cover art.

Caravan to America

Living Arts of the Silk Road

John S. Major and Betty J. Belanus

CRICKET BOOKS / A MARCATO BOOK
CHICAGO

Grateful acknowledgment is made to the following individuals: Zahir Abdul, Marc Aronson, Steve Brown, Marina Budhos, Joëlle Dujardin, Merrill Feather, Zev Feldman, Yung Ho, Maggie Holtzburg, Rich Kennedy, Karen Kohn, Theodore Levin, Cecilia Pang, Carol Saller, Stephanie Smith, John Tebobian, Shu-Ni Tsou, Chris Walter, and Esther Won.

Design by Karen Kohn
Production by Cara Dermyer and Walter Mendoza
A Note on the Design: Each chapter features patterns
and motifs authentic to the cultures described. The use of
symmetrical designs within circles, intertwining leaves, and
fanciful animals are common.

Library of Congress Cataloging-in-Publication Data
Major, John S.
  Caravan to America : living arts of the silk road / John S. Major and Betty J. Belanus.-- 1st ed.
      p. cm.
  "A Marcato book."
Summary: Profiles eight artists and artisans now living in America who are originally from the "Silk Road," an ancient network of caravan trails through which trade goods, ideas, and arts pass between Asia and the Mediterranean. Includes bibliographical references and index.
     ISBN 0-8126-2666-4 (alk. paper) -- ISBN 0-8126-2677-X (pbk. : alk. paper)
1. Folk art — Asia, Central — Juvenile literature. 2. Ethnic art — Asia, Central — Juvenile literature. 3. Handicraft — Asia, Central — Juvenile literature. 4. Expatriate artists — United States — Juvenile literature. 5. Folk artists — Asia, Central — Juvenile literature. 6. Artisans — Asia, Central — Juvenile literature. 7. Arts, American — 20th century — Juvenile literature. [1. Folk art — Asia, Central. 2. Handicraft — Asia, Central. 3. Artists. 4. Artisans.] I. Belanus, Betty J. II. Title.
  NX575 .C37 2002
  745'.089'95073 — dc21
                              2002005477

Contents

Foreword

After twenty-five years of performing the cello in different parts of the world, I have learned how effectively music speaks to people everywhere, despite what at first might seem like very great cultural differences. When people travel, they bring their own music; and wherever they go, they are intrigued by the music they hear. Many aspects of music, including distinctive instruments, scales, and melodies have moved from culture to culture with ease.

As with music, people are the product of all the cultures they experience. I am no exception. My parents came from China to live in France, where I was born. We moved to New York when I was seven years old, and I now live in Boston with my family.

People from diverse backgrounds find different ways to talk to each other—music plays a big part in that conversation. As a result of my musical travels, I began to think about the exchange that occurred along the historic Silk Road, the ancient network of caravan trails that for more than two thousand years connected Asia to the Mediterranean and beyond. In addition to trading items such as silk from China and glassware from Persia along this route, travelers engaged in a lively exchange of ideas and arts.

In 1998, we started the Silk Road Project to share and explore the rich cultural traditions of the peoples of the Silk Road. Later, we founded the Silk Road Ensemble, a chamber music group that includes musicians from such countries as Armenia, Azerbaijan, China, India, Iran,

Japan, Korea, Mongolia, Turkey, Tadjikistan, and Uzbekistan. Performing traditional music as well as new compositions, these musicians are equally versed in musical knowledge past and present, cosmopolitan and traditional.

This book is about history, not just the past, but history as it is happening right now. It is about history that continues from the past into the present and is being preserved for the future.

The artists and craftspeople featured in this book all have family backgrounds in the countries of the Silk Road. The families of some have been in America now for several generations; others were born in Asia or Europe and came to this country as immigrants. All practice arts that have deep roots in their home countries. By continuing to perform their music, cook their food, and paint their pictures, they are preserving their heritage in a new land. But by practicing their arts in America, they are also agents of change. Their arts are made known to people who might never have encountered them. At the same time, these arts have evolved in new ways influenced by the many cultures and traditions that make up the tapestry of American life.

This type of cultural exchange is similar to that of the historic Silk Road, where people traveling in caravans traded, told stories, played music, and shared new ideas and ways of doing things. The travelers of the Silk Road practiced their native cultures wherever they went and took pleasure in the new cultures they encountered on their journeys.

As the world grows smaller, people continue to be curious about other cultures, whether they are to be found halfway around the globe or halfway down the block. It has never been easier to explore the richness of the world's cultures. These stories provide a window into the living arts of the world.

Yo-Yo Ma

Introduction

*History is a mirror of the past
And a lesson for the present.*
　　　　　—*Persian proverb*

Yeshi Dorjee paints intricate thangkas on silk. Najmieh Batmanglij teaches gourmet cooks how to bake fragrant baklava. Peter Kyvelos builds beautiful ouds. Qi Shu Fang dazzles audiences as the female star of a Peking opera called *The Legend of the White Snake.*

Thangkas, baklava, ouds, and Peking opera are only a few of the things you'll read about in this book. What ties all of these arts and their makers together? All of these people, and the other four you'll learn about, carry on traditions here in America that had their beginnings along the Silk Road.

The term "Silk Road" was invented in the nineteenth century to describe a series of ancient routes along which goods, including silk made in China, were traded. Some items, such as glass, went mostly east from Italy to East Asia, and others, such as spices and paper (and of course silk), went east to west. The Silk Road was actually not one route, but many. The way was dangerous and difficult: travelers encountered high mountains,

Caravan travelers cook a meal in this sixteenth-century Persian watercolor.

hot deserts, bandits, hostile armies, and wild animals. Few traders traveled the entire distance between China and the Mediterranean; rather, they went part of the way, sold their goods, and returned home again. Trade items often changed hands several times on their long journey.

Ideas, religions, foods, music, and languages were also traded and shared as people encountered each other. Great empires battled one another for strategic territories along the Silk Road, and each wave of invasion exposed people to new forms of art and culture.

Roman men in the age of the Caesars complained about the cost of the Chinese silk that their wives liked to wear. In eighth-century China, conservative men grumbled that young women had adopted a fashion for Turkish-style tight jackets and liked to play such unladylike Central Asian sports as polo. Paper, invented in China around 100 B.C., was being made in the Central Asian city of Samarkand in the eighth century A.D. and gave a big boost to the spread of literacy in the expanding Islamic world. In Korea in the 1430s, a water-powered mechanical clock was constructed for King Sejong's Royal Observatory; the basic operating system of the clock can be traced to a Arabic book published in Syria in 1206. Despite distance, danger, and hardship, the Silk Road knitted the ancient world together in remarkably complex ways.

The people featured in this book have roots all along the Silk Road, from Greece to Korea, and the arts they practice are just as varied. The artists do have a lot in common, though. They all have a strong feeling for their homelands, or those of their parents or grandparents. These feelings of attachment are very evident when Khaliq Muradi, for example, talks about how his mother would slowly cook a stew back home in Afghanistan by burying the pot under the family campfire.

Other common traits of these artists are an enthusiasm for and a deep commitment to their arts. For all of them, art is not just a creative outlet or a way to make a living. It's part of who they are, a part of their very being. In the words of the Bukharan Jewish poet Ilyas Malayev, who now leads a New York musical group that Tamara Katayev performs with, "If a nation can preserve its musical heritage, and thereby its culture, then such a nation is forever alive."

A third thing they have in common is the desire to pass on their art through teaching, performing, demonstrating, writing, and exhibiting. That's why they are all excited about this book. They want to share their traditions with you, let you catch their excitement about what they do, and try out some activities related to their arts.

As you read each chapter, you will learn a bit about the ancient and modern histories of places all along the Silk Road and the background of each artistic tradition. But the heart of each chapter is the story of the people behind the arts, the people who carry within them a spark of the Silk Road—an ember of the rich artistic heritage of their homelands—and nurture the flame in their new homes.

Like the antique woven rugs that Khaliq Muradi repairs, the arts carried on by each of these people have taken on some changes as they are transplanted to America. Be on the lookout for these changes as you read along. But as Khaliq says, "A fine antique rug is too precious to allow it to wear out. If you restore it too much, you can kill its spirit. What you want to do is stabilize and protect the rug, but not to alter its personality." Through the work of the people in this book, the spirit of Silk Road arts lives on in America.

Qi Shu Fang
Peking Opera Performer

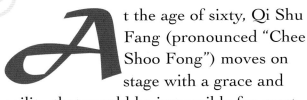

At the age of sixty, Qi Shu Fang (pronounced "Chee Shoo Fong") moves on stage with a grace and agility that would be impossible for most twenty-year-olds. In a recent performance in New York in the title role of the Chinese opera *Mu Gui Ying,* she plays a woman warrior who takes command of a Chinese army to defeat an enemy invasion; the play is based on a historical incident from nearly a thousand years ago. Ms. Qi is at center stage, preparing to do battle. She twirls a long spear in faster and faster and more and more complex patterns, then juggles a pair of swords while waiting for the enemy to attack. The enemy soldiers rush her, one after another; she flings them to the ground with a dazzling series of martial arts throws. They stand off and throw spears at her; she sends them flying back, rebounding off her hands, her feet, her own spear, even her back. Finally she whirls in a circle, sweeping the stage with her spear; the last remaining enemies go tumbling and leaping away, leaving her victorious. Needless to say, the audience goes wild.

From Peking to New York

When Qi Shu Fang first came to America in May 1988, she had nothing more in mind than to spend a few months visiting friends in New York before returning home to China. "In China I was famous as a leading star of Peking Opera," she recalls. "My career was very secure and I had toured abroad several times to perform in Europe and Japan. I had no reason to consider moving to the United States, or anywhere else."

She had not been in New York very long when she began to change her mind. To start with, she was surprised to learn that there was not one single professional Peking Opera troupe in America, despite the large size of the Chinese American community. There were a number of amateur troupes, though, and she found herself besieged with requests to perform with them or give workshops. And she

Qi Shu Fang as Duke Iron Fan at the Polish Festival of Arts, 2000

Peking or Beijing?

Many people think that the name of China's capital changed a few years ago from Peking to Beijing. But the Chinese name did not change at all; what changed was the way the name is commonly spelled in English. There are many systems of using the Roman alphabet to spell Chinese words; in the 1960s, the government of the People's Republic of China began promoting the use of a phonetic system called pinyin. "Peking" is the old Western spelling adopted by the British Post Office in the late nineteenth century; "Beijing" is the same word spelled in pinyin. Either way, the Chinese term means, literally, "northern capital." "Peking Opera" and "Beijing Opera" are just two different ways of saying the same thing.

Program for the
2001 Peking Opera
Festival, New York

was amazed by the interest in Peking opera that she found, not only among Chinese Americans but also in the wider American performing arts community. So she wound up postponing her return to China several times in order to satisfy her growing number of American fans.

The key moment came in October 1988, when she performed with members of an amateur opera troupe at Pace University in New York City, a campus located just a few blocks from Chinatown. Most people in the audience had some familiarity with traditional Peking opera, but for many, the martial arts style that Ms. Qi had made her specialty was something entirely new. In the audience was a famous Columbia University professor of Chinese literature, C. T. Hsia, who later was quoted in a newspaper as saying that Ms. Qi's performance was the best he had seen in forty or fifty years.

"Of course I was very proud of that," she says. "But even better, it got a lot of people's attention."

Soon after that performance, the World Music Institute sponsored a full-scale performance of one of Ms. Qi's favorite operas, *The Legend of the White Snake,* at Manhattan's Symphony Space theater. This time the audience was ethnically mixed, but mostly not Chinese American, proving that the demand for Peking opera in America reached beyond traditional audiences. Spurred by this enthusiastic response, Qi Shu Fang decided to move permanently to New York and organize America's first professional Chinese opera company. Since 1988, the Qi Shu Fang Peking Opera Company, managed by Ms. Qi's husband and costar Ding Mei Kui, has put on dozens of performances in New York and around the country, as well as many workshops and courses for performers who want to learn the techniques of Peking opera.

What is Chinese Opera?

Peking (or Beijing) opera is one of many regional variations of the popular musical theater of China. The Chinese words *qu* or *xi* are both usually translated into English as "opera," but Chinese opera is not very much like the European opera long familiar to Western audiences; the Chinese terms really mean something more like "musical theater." (But we will continue to use the word "opera" here, because it has become so familiar.) Like Western opera, Chinese opera uses many different theatrical devices to tell a story, usually a romance, a fantasy fable, or a historical tale. Singing is a much less central part of Chinese opera, where performers also communicate by spoken dialogue, mime, dance, acrobatics, and martial arts. The performers' costumes and makeup are typically very elaborate, but the sets and props are usually very simple. Actors are expected to be able to make the audience visualize places and things through their mime and dancing, rather than using realistic scenery and actual objects. All of the action of a performance, including singing, is accompanied by an orchestra (as few as four players or as many as a dozen), which includes the *erhu* (Chinese violin), *sona* (Chinese oboe), cymbals, blocks, drums, and other percussion, and perhaps other woodwinds and strings.

Chinese opera dates back at least to the Tang Dynasty (618–907), and flourished under the Yuan Dynasty (1279–1368), when China was ruled by Kubilai Khan and other Mongol emperors. Many of the best operas were written during the Yuan Dynasty or the subsequent Ming Dynasty (1368–1644). Their stories, songs, and dialogue are as familiar to Chinese opera fans as *Aida* or *Madame Butterfly* would be to opera fans in the West.

Opera performers, Shanghai, 1870

Tradition and Change

As was true in England in Shakespeare's time, women were not allowed to perform on stage in premodern China. Although the rule was not always enforced, generally speaking all parts in Chinese opera were played by men, and some actors specialized in roles as female impersonators. But this began to change around the middle of the twentieth century, when a number of influential figures in Chinese opera (including the superstar Mei Lanfang, famous for his skill in playing female roles) felt that it was necessary to modernize Chinese opera somewhat to maintain its popularity in changing times.

By then Ms. Qi had already begun her training as an opera performer, starting at the age of four. She soon showed the outstanding talent that would make her career so successful. She came to the attention of M Lanfang himself; wi as her mentor, she b an eager proponent of t ern performance style. "Fror

Qi Shu Fang fighting off attackers in *The Legend of the White Snake*

beginning, I was not very interested in romantic roles," she says with a hearty laugh. "I specialized in 'woman warrior' martial arts roles, or else the kinds of fresh, witty young women who contrasted with the softer romantic heroines."

Qi Shu Fang as Chang Bao, the heroic woodcutter's daughter, in *Taking Tiger Mountain by Strategy*

Her big break came in the mid-1960s, during a period of radical cultural experimentation in China. The Communist government (prodded by the wife of Chairman Mao Zedong, who was very interested in arts reform) declared that traditional operas were too old-fashioned and politically unacceptable, and could no longer be performed. Instead, eight "revolutionary operas" were created, and Qi Shu Fang won the leading female role in one of them. *Taking Tiger Mountain by Strategy* tells of a squad of revolutionary army soldiers who need to capture a mountain held by bandits. They are not able to do so until they are helped by Chang Bao, the daughter of a local woodcutter, who knows the mountain well and is able to show the soldiers how to attack its weakest point. Ms. Qi's performance was praised by Madame Mao and many others, and she became a national celebrity.

Qi Shu Fang (right, with sash) with China's Premier Zhou Enlai and Chairman Mao Zedong, c. 1970

After the death of Mao Zedong in 1976, traditional operas gradually came back to the Chinese stage, and Ms. Qi added other famous roles as women warriors to her repertoire. But in some ways Chang Bao remains her signature role; in 1998, in a performance at Pace University to mark the tenth anniversary of her New York troupe, she again played the heroic woodcutter's daughter to huge acclaim.

The Qi Shu Fang Peking Opera Company taking a curtain call

An Evolving Art

Ms. Qi continues to work to make Chinese opera as appealing as possible to modern audiences. Her performances all feature projected subtitles in English so that everyone can follow the songs and the dialogue. She noticed that American audiences at Chinese opera performances easily become bored with long passages of singing, especially because the singing style of Chinese opera is quite unfamiliar in the West. "So I've shortened the songs in my performances, and I emphasize dance, acrobatics, and martial arts, which are very popular." But she also knows that both Chinese and non-Chinese American audiences want tradition and authenticity as well as excitement, and she is careful not to tinker with the plots of the classical operas, or to compromise standards of quality. Her work sets the standard for Chinese opera performances in this country, and other stars push themselves hard to reach a comparable standard of skill and artistry.

Her troupe's performances are truly collaborative. She has her costumes and sets made in China and shipped to the United States. Most of her lead actors and actresses are Chinese, trained in classical performance techniques, who have come to America especially to join the Qi Shu Fang Peking Opera Company. "But some members of my troupe are Americans, not of Chinese ancestry," she says, proud of these young performers whom she has trained herself. And she adds, with a smile, "With makeup on, you can't tell anyway."

Like Tamara Katayev and Khaliq Muradi, also profiled in this book, Ms. Qi and her husband live in Queens, one of five boroughs that make up the City of New York, and the most ethnically diverse county in the United States. "I had it very easy as a Chinese immigrant," she says. "No restaurant work, no garment work like most Chinese newcomers. I was able to practice my own profession full time, right away." In addition to a demanding performance schedule, she gives many workshops, lectures, and classes. Her one regret so far is that she can't establish a Chinese opera school here that would train children in opera techniques from a very young age, as was the tradition in China. "Not so many American parents would want this for their children," she says. "I think I will still have to get performers from China for a long time." Then she adds, brightening again, "But I give lots of demonstrations in schools, and the children love it. I think they will be part of the audience for Chinese opera in the future."

The sheer theatricality and entertainment value of Chinese opera has ensured a steady and appreciative audience not only for Qi Shu Fang's troupe but also for an increasing number of visiting troupes from mainland China and Taiwan. "When I first arrived here," says Ms. Qi, "I thought that there was a chance for me to do something really important. And I think I have done that now. I believe that Chinese opera has a very good future in America."

Qi Shu Fang visiting a New York City public scho

Doug Kim
*Korean American
Martial Artist*

ook under "martial arts" in the yellow pages in any American city, and you're likely to find aikido, hapkido, judo, jujitsu, karate, kendo, taekwondo, and others. How did these ancient Asian arts of discipline and self-defense become so popular in America, and what can they teach us?

Doug Kim is a good person to ask. Doug, who lives near San Francisco, California, has been seriously involved in Asian martial arts for almost thirty years. His parents came from Korea before he was born, and Doug took his first martial arts lessons when he was in fifth grade. His skill is apparent when he demonstrates some impressive moves. His enthusiasm spills out when he explains the many lessons he has learned from martial arts. But he's also quick to tell you that, even after years and years of training and practice, he's just an advanced beginner.

The Origins of Asian Martial Arts

According to Doug's research, there are many different Asian martial arts with distinct origins and unique characteristics. They do, however, have a common goal: combining self-defense and self-discipline skills.

Around 520 A.D., a Buddhist monk named Bodhidharma (Ta-mo in Chinese and Daruma in Japanese) traveled from India to China, eventually stopping at a temple called Shaolin in Honan Province. Trained since childhood as a warrior, he is said to have developed eighteen exercises (called "Eighteen Hands of Lohan") to improve the Shaolin monks' ability to endure long meditation sessions. These exercises evolved into Shaolin boxing and strongly influenced other Chinese martial arts. Shaolin martial arts became what is now often called kung fu. Shaolin monasteries, although in remote locations, were

Bodhidharma

Wooden guardian figures from a temple in Japan, now at the entrance of the Freer Gallery at the Smithsonian Institution

often centers of learning and wealth and were also sanctuaries for battle-weary soldiers and political refugees. Over time, Doug explains, they became incubators of effective and proven fighting techniques.

"It might seem curious that lethal fighting arts were developed and practiced by religious men," Doug admits. "But the Shaolin monks needed martial arts to improve their ability to meditate and defend themselves against road bandits, temple robbers, and periodic government persecution. Study and use of martial arts were important not only to spiritual development but to survival." Other martial arts had unique roots in other Asian countries, including Japan, Okinawa, and Korea, but Chinese styles became highly influential throughout Asia. "Chinese guards for hire protected merchants along the Silk Road; Shaolin missionaries carried Buddhism to Korea and Japan; and professional soldiers

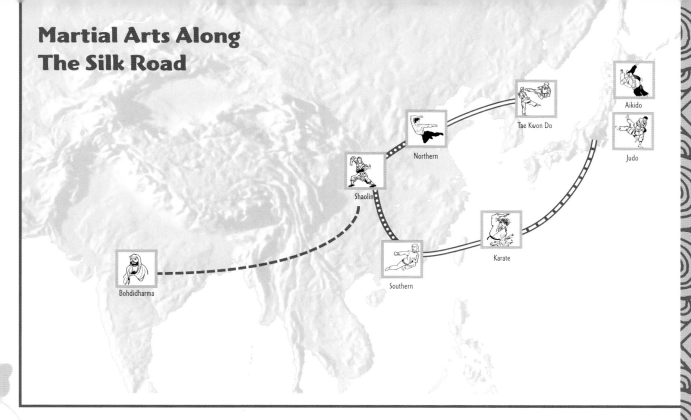

Martial Arts Along The Silk Road

Bohdidharma

Shaolin

Northern

Southern

Karate

Tae Kwon Do

Aikido

Judo

adopted effective foreign [Chinese/ Shaolin] techniques," Doug says.

Doug points out evidence of Chinese influence in the language of Asian martial arts. Chinese characters were the most predominant form of communication in the region, and the characters origi-nally used in Okinawa for "karate" liter-ally mean: "Chinese hand way." The same characters are used for the Korean mar-tial art tang soo do. Bodhidharma's meditation traveled all the way from India to Japan, forming the basis for Zen Buddhism as well as the samurai tradition.

Asian Martial Arts in America

A few Americans did take an interest in Asian martial arts, Doug says, as early as the 1900s. "In 1902, President Teddy Roosevelt began taking judo lessons from a Japanese, but for the most part Asian martial arts remained invisible to the general public for decades. After World War II, American servicemen returning from the Pacific became interested in the fighting skills they had seen. But the real floodgates of interest didn't open until Bruce Lee's kung fu movies hit the U.S. in the 1970s," Doug explains. "Virtually overnight, kung fu, judo, karate, taekwondo, and wushu schools, clubs, movies, and competitions became part of American life. Both judo and taekwondo are now Olympic sports, and wushu might be added in the future. Martial arts techniques once taught in

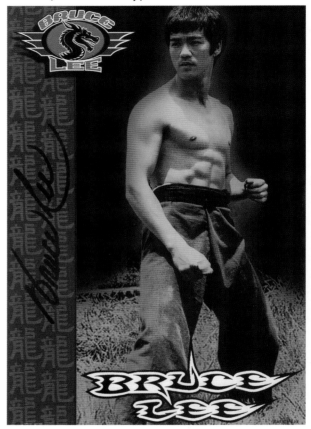

Legendary martial artist Bruce Lee appeared in many films in the 1970s.

secret only to blood relatives—and never to non-Asians—are now taught openly to anyone interested in learning."

Doug Kim sparring with partner Steve Brown

Doug Kim's Personal Journey

Doug Kim's involvement in the martial arts came as part of a journey of self-discovery. When he was growing up, his family followed many Korean customs: they ate traditional Korean foods and celebrated Korean holidays. His parents spoke Korean to each other, were proud of their native country, and often (it seemed to Doug) disciplined their four children more strictly than his friends' parents did. Yet Doug felt that his parents, who had moved to the United States when they were in their early twenties, could never really explain what it meant to be "Korean."

While his father was studying to be a surgeon, the Kims moved around the Midwestern United States about every five years. They were usually the only Asian family in their area. Other children would taunt Doug and his siblings, calling them "Chink" and "Jap." "I would say, 'No, I'm Korean' and we'd fight about it and I'd get beaten up," Doug recalls.

When the family moved to Munster, Indiana, in the 1960s, neighborhood kids didn't like the "new Asian kids on the block." Doug and his brother got beaten up often. Doug's dad decided that his sons needed to learn some self-defense, so he

Doug Kim and Steve Brown
demonstrating hapkido moves

24

took them to nearby Hammond, Indiana, for six months of judo lessons.

The family moved to Farmington, Michigan, outside Detroit, in 1971. "By that time, taekwondo had become known in the United States, and a few schools opened up. I remember trying to get a taekwondo club started at my high school, but there weren't enough people interested." Doug's grandfather came to visit and introduced him to a taekwondo master in Detroit, but Doug couldn't arrange transportation to take lessons.

Finally, in the summer of 1974, Doug got to study taekwondo on his first visit to Korea, after graduating from high school. (Such a trip is customary in many Korean American families, Doug explains.) "We went to a very modest gym that was over a machine shop. It had one broken fan, rather primitive wooden floors, and excellent training. We sweated a lot!"

Doug continued learning taekwondo while at the University of Michigan, where he majored in East Asian studies.

"I studied Chinese, Japanese, Asian history, religion, philosophy, art, and basically for the first time in my life had important aspects of my Korean identity explained to me in English—in terms I could understand." He returned to Korea for a longer visit in 1978 after graduating from college, to get some firsthand experience in all that he had learned about Asia in college. While in Korea, he studied taekwondo six days a week, two hours a day. "I began as a white belt when I got to Korea in '74, but I had to start all over again in '78. I worked hard and took my black belt test around Easter of 1979."

In 1981 when he moved to Chicago to start a career in banking, Doug began studying hapkido, another Korean martial art, which he describes as "the Swiss army knife of martial arts, kind of a grab bag of styles."

Beyond the First-Level Black Belt

After Doug received his first-level black belt, he continued training. It's a common misunderstanding, Doug explains, that receiving a black belt is the ultimate achievement in martial arts. There are up to ten degrees of black belt in some martial arts. "First-degree black belt, or first 'dan,' just means you are an advanced beginner—with many basic skills beginning to sink in."

It may take as long to get to second-dan (degree) black belt as it did to get from the very beginning of training to first dan. The training for each dan level gets harder, and the time to achieve the next level can get longer. "As you advance, you're judged not only on your technical proficiency but on your maturity and your leadership, because you become more of an example to others."

Belts of different colors symbolize levels of expertise in many martial arts.

This might seem frustrating to Americans, who want everything quickly, Doug says. "True mastery of the skills and objectives of martial arts are more of a lifetime pursuit than something that comes in just a few years. The study of martial arts is a marathon, not a sprint—you have to take the long view."

It's Not Just Fighting

Many people get the idea from watching movies and television that Asian martial arts are only about fighting, but Doug says true martial artists do not fight unless they absolutely must defend themselves.

Martial arts training is more about self-discipline. "Ultimately, the objective of martial arts is to conquer only your-self." Because of the great potential for injury in martial arts training, mutual respect and courtesy are taught alongside the techniques. At the beginning of a mar-tial arts class, and before numerous exercises, students bow to each other. "It's a formal way of say-ing, 'Please take care of me,

please respect me—and I will do the same for you.'"
At the beginning and end of class, students bow to their instructors and seniors.

Students must practice martial arts moves over and over again, like playing scales on an instrument, to learn "bone deep" as Doug puts it. "Practice, practice, practice, persevere, persevere, persevere, and measure improvement by degrees. These things—character development, mutual respect, focus, attention span—are all transfer-able to other parts of our lives and endeavors."

Doug says, "Martial arts are one of the best ways to develop the union of mind, body, and spirit. The ability to unify your mind and your body to accomplish tasks is crucial to all aspects of life. Whether you are Yo-Yo Ma playing cello, an Olympic ice skater, or a student taking a math test, it's the same concentration, the same focus."

The Journey Continues

Doug Kim currently holds black belts in taekwondo and hapkido. He has served as an assistant instructor, but until he reaches his fourth dan, he will not officially be instructor grade.

Some recent knee surgery has set back his training, but he still hopes to test for third dan this year and fourth dan by the time he turns fifty, about five years from now. By then his twin children, a boy and girl, will be ten years old, and he wants to formally teach them martial arts. "I'll be able to teach them as their instructor, not just as their dad, and pass along this aspect of our rich Korean heritage."

This goal is in keeping with Doug's explanation of true achievement in the Asian martial arts, which is as ancient as the beginnings of these arts along the Silk Road: "The benefit actually comes from training, from the work, from striving . . . the point is that the journey is more important than the destination."

Yeshi Dorjee
Tibetan Artist-Monk

Yeshi Dorjee sits in his small, simply furnished room at the Land of Compassion Buddha Center near Los Angeles, radiating the air of friendly self-confidence that seems to be the trademark quality of Buddhist monks. "I had a very hard time in the first year of my life," he says, smiling. "My mother was already pregnant with me when she and my father fled from Tibet in 1960." The Chinese army had invaded Tibet the year before, and it was a terrible time for Tibetans. The Dalai Lama, their spiritual leader, had escaped to India, and hundreds of thousands of Tibetans had followed him into exile. Yeshi's parents settled in Bhutan, a small, isolated country in the Himalaya Mountains, between Tibet and the northeastern border of India. "Bhutan is where I was born. But then my father died when I was only seven months old. I have no memory of him. I think things were difficult for my mother."

All of that seems far in the past now. Yeshi is a fully ordained Buddhist monk—

hi Dorjee
n the *Green*
a thangka

his proper title is the
Venerable Yeshi Dorjee—
and he has been in the
United States since 1997,
living as a guest at the
Land of Compassion
Buddha community and
sharing his knowledge of
Buddhist sacred art
with Buddhist temples
and communities across
America. He recently
completed a project that
was very important to
him, painting the story
of the life of the
Buddha in a series of
forty-one thangkas.

What is a thangka?

A thangka (pronounced "tahng-kah")
is a Tibetan Buddhist religious painting;
the word refers to the type of painting,
not to its subject matter. A thangka is

The Path of Meditation, by Yeshi Dorjee

An Illustrated Meditation Story

One thangka that Yeshi painted to keep in his own room is an illustrated lesson on how to meditate. The painting shows a monk, an elephant, a monkey, and a long, winding upward path. The monk represents the person who is setting out on the path of learning to meditate. The elephant is his mind—at first gray, heavy, and hard to move. The elephant, we see, is led at first by the monkey, which represents the tendency to become distracted. As an Indian proverb puts it, "A monkey never stays for long in the same tree."

As the path winds upward, it passes symbols of the senses—flowers for smell, fruit for taste, musical instruments for sound, and so on. The monk has to learn to ignore all of these in meditation, and gradually he begins to succeed: the elephant of his mind is becoming purified, changing from a muddy, heavy gray to a pure, shining gold, a little at a time.

Finally the monk reaches his goal of perfect meditation, and his purified, meditative mind has become completely harmonious. In the end the monk seems to leave his body altogether to explore the realm of purely spiritual matters.

The thirteenth Dalai Lama's favorite artist painting a thangka in 1937

painted to hang on a wall, usually mounted in a cloth frame made of brocade or some other fancy fabric. It is designed to be displayed and looked at and used as a part of daily religious life.

Thangkas, Yeshi explains, are made for many reasons. You can paint one or commission a monk to paint one for you, as an act of religious merit, in the hope of gaining some benefit, such as long life or a favorable rebirth in a new life for a deceased parent. Commissioning a thangka can be a way of expressing regret for having done something bad. Or a person confronting a bad situation, such as an illness, might be advised by a monk to have

Pen-and-ink drawing by Yeshi Dorjee, in preparation for painting a thangka

a thangka painted as a way of changing his bad fortune. A thangka is also a good gift for a friend who needs spiritual encouragement. Sometimes a new thangka is created when a high lama (Tibetan Buddhist monk) has a religious vision and describes it to a monk-painter to make into a painting. "Traditionally," Yeshi explains, "a lot depended on how much money a patron had to spend on making the thangka, for example to buy expensive pigments and gold leaf. A thangka could be simple or elaborate, depending on the wishes of the person who ordered it."

For whatever reason they are painted, thangkas are mainly aids to meditation; they help focus the mind's inner eye. (Meditation, which is a key religious practice in Buddhism, means more than just deep thinking. It is a disciplined way of emptying the mind of all conscious thought and distractions, so as to make room for unconscious religious truth.) For

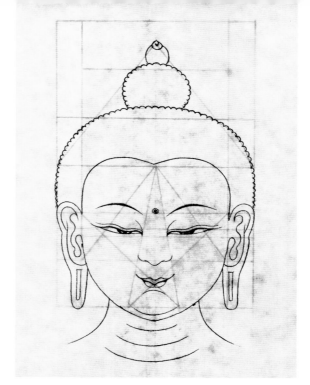

A grid system is used by Tibetan artists to assure that proportions are correct.

example, Yeshi keeps in his room a thangka of Green Tara, a goddess who symbolizes the compassion of the Buddha. Compassion, the quality of being kind to and caring deeply about all living things, is one of the most important virtues in Buddhism. So meditating on the Green

Yeshi ready to
start painting a
new thangka

Tara thangka is a way of increasing one's own capacity for compassion.

As a Buddhist monk, Yeshi has many duties and obligations, but painting thangkas is what he likes to do most. Completing the series of forty-one thangkas of the Buddha's life has been an important spiritual journey for him. He also sees it as a way of contributing to the happiness of others by helping them to understand Buddhism better. Like monks, priests, and imams of other religions, he has devoted his life to sharing spiritual insight with others.

The Path of an Artist-Monk

After a difficult beginning, Yeshi had quite a happy childhood in Bhutan. His mother remarried and had more children, and Yeshi felt comfortable at home and in primary school. From a very early age, he liked to draw pictures as a way of relaxing from his schoolwork. Then, at the age of nine, he came home from school one day and announced to his mother that he had decided to become a Buddhist monk.

Yeshi's mother tried to discourage him by pointing out all of the difficulties he would face. For starters, how would he get to India, where the main Tibetan Buddhist universities-in-exile are located? One of Yeshi's uncles questioned him closely about his decision, to see whether he was truly serious. When he was fully convinced, he told Yeshi that he would sponsor him to study in India if he could get his mother's permission. "After I asked her many times, I wore down her resistance," Yeshi says, laughing. "So she finally said O.K." Soon afterward, he began his studies at Gyudmed Tantric University in Karnataka, India. He would be a student there for the next twenty-five years.

The curriculum at the university was designed especially to train Buddhist monks and is quite different from what one would expect at an American university. In addition to Tibetan literature, grammar, and writing, there are five major areas of study:

1. Perfection of wisdom (sacred texts and theology)
2. Logic and debate
3. Philosophy
4. Theories of reality
5. Monastic ritual, chanting, and discipline

After twenty years, Yeshi was promoted from advanced student to assistant professor. After five more years, in 1995, he passed his final examinations (which involved, he recalls, memorizing a huge amount of material) and was awarded a *ngag-ram-pa* (Ph.D.) degree with honors. In addition to all of his other studies, Yeshi had become expert in many of the specialized arts of Tibetan Buddhism, including thangka painting, butter sculpture, sand mandalas, and calligraphy. (His hobby is also in the fine arts: he is a very accomplished photographer.) Having finished his studies, he decided to stay on at Gyudmed University as head of its department of ritual arts. But as it turned out, he did not stay there long.

One of Yeshi's special skills is making mandalas. "The word mandala in Sanskrit [the ancient classical language of India] means 'circle,' and a mandala is a kind of symbolic spiritual map of the whole universe." he explains. "A mandala is a way of visualizing reality." So mandalas can be

Left and below: Monks from the Namgyai monastery in Dharamsala, India, creating an intricate sand mandala at the Smithsonian Folklife Festival in 2000

painted as thangkas, but not all thangkas are mandalas.

The most basic form of a mandala is a set of concentric circles (representing different levels of the heavens) containing a set of concentric squares (representing the earth), usually all filled with sacred symbolic figures. Mandalas can be done as paintings, but they can be created in many other ways as well—sometimes even buildings are designed as mandalas. One type of mandala that has special significance in Tibet is the sand mandala, "painted" on a table or other flat surface with many different colors of sand. The sand is added to the picture with special spoons and funnels; the work has to be done very carefully because there is no way to correct mistakes. A large and complex sand mandala can take many weeks to complete. When one is finished, it is used as the focus of a religious ceremony and then immediately destroyed by sweeping the sand away.

The important thing is the spiritual discipline of making the mandala; in Buddhism, an attachment to physical things—such as wanting to keep the sand mandala instead of sweeping it away—is considered an obstacle to spiritual enlightenment.

Coming to America

Yeshi's exceptional talents as a practitioner of Buddhist ritual arts soon won him a growing reputation. He was awarded first prize in an exhibition of Tibetan calligraphy that drew entries from all over South Asia. The office of the Dalai Lama commissioned several thangkas from him and then praised the results. Yeshi's skills at sculpting religious statues from colored butter and of making mandalas from colored sand made him a welcome guest when ceremonies were conducted at Buddhist temples. Soon his reputation reached the United States.

In 1996, Yeshi received an invitation from the Gyuto Wheel of Dharma Monastery in Minneapolis to come as a visitor and teacher, for as long as he wished to stay. He arrived in America in 1997 and has lived in this country ever since, staying at one Buddhist monastery

Yeshi showing a thangka to His Holiness the Dalai Lama

or study center after another. As a monk, Yeshi owns very few possessions, and has no need of a house or an apartment; his home is with whatever religious community invites him to stay.

Yeshi was at first surprised, then delighted, by the amount of freedom he found in America. The Tibetans who fled to India in 1959 to escape the Chinese occupation of Tibet are still regarded by the Indian government as refugees and temporary guests; they have to be careful of what they say and do. The freedom to believe and practice religion without interference is very precious to Yeshi, and he hopes to stay in America from now on. His strongest wish is to create a Buddhist arts center in America, where he can teach thangka painting and the other arts that he knows so well. He would like especially to introduce Buddhist arts to American children.

In the past fifty years or so, Buddhism has slowly but surely grown in America to become one of the country's mainstream religions, and not just among people of Asian descent. People from all over the country, and from other countries as well, visit communities like the Land of Compassion Buddha for periods of a few weeks to several years to study Buddhist teachings; there seems to be a strong demand for the kinds of lessons that Yeshi knows how to teach. There are still problems to solve before his school of Buddhist religious arts becomes a reality—such basics as a location, funding, and other teachers are still uncertain—but he is confident that all such obstacles will be overcome.

Detail of flowers from one of Yeshi's thangkas

Meanwhile, I asked, does he have any American students of thangka painting now? "I have one student about to begin," he replied. "Up until now I have been very busy painting full time, and also it has been hard to find students who can make the necessary commitment of time. It takes ten years to learn to paint thangkas properly." Then he reconsidered, and added, "Actually, it is not so hard to paint thangkas. Anyone with professional art training could learn to do it in a few weeks. What takes so long is knowing what to put in each thangka. The content is the hard part, not the technique."

I asked him to explain that some more. "Suppose I decided to do a series of paintings of American presidents," he said. "To start with, I would have to include all of them, from George Washington to President Bush. Then, for each of them there are certain things I would have to include to show their place in history. But

I would also have a lot of freedom to paint as I wished. Thangka painting is just like that. You have to know what must be included, and also where it is good to exercise your own artistic vision. There is a lot of freedom in terms of style and decoration, but each thangka must be correct in terms of its religious message. It has to be something that tells a story and teaches a lesson. That's why I say that the art training is easy, but the Buddhist training is not easy."

As I leave the Land of Compassion Buddha community to start on my trip home, Yeshi gives me a piece of paper inscribed with a sacred text and tied with colored string, to protect me on the journey, along with a set of Buddhist prayer beads and a white silk prayer scarf as a blessing. I go away feeling deeply moved by the spirituality and wisdom of this quiet, polite, sweet-tempered, and profoundly good man.

One of Yeshi's series of forty-one thangkas of the life of the Buddha

Abdul Khaliq Muradi
Turkmen Rug Restorer

Abdul Khaliq Muradi (everyone calls him Khaliq, pronounced "Ha-Luk") greets me at the door to the Antique Rug Gallery on "Decorator's Row" in midtown Manhattan and shoves aside the large, heavy rug he has been working on. It has a beautiful floral design in soft colors of green, tan, and rose, but it also looks rather odd. Bare patches show through in some places, while in others the surface is shaggy and rough, like an untrimmed beard. "This rug was woven in Belgium or France around 1800," says Khaliq. "It is a very good piece, very valuable, but as you see, it is badly damaged, too. It was brought in by some people from Boston, whose family owned it since it was new."

He points out some of the problems. "Here it was folded for a long time, and the weave has cracked. This part was in front of a sofa, maybe; it is worn almost through to the floor." I asked him what he was doing to repair it. "Of course I

A typical
Turkmen rug

49

Late nineteenth-century Turkmens in typical dress. The seated man wears the costume of the emir of Bukhara.

recognized the knots and the type of yarn right away," he answered. "That comes from experience. So I started by matching the colors and the weight of the yarn and then made some decisions about what to repair and what to leave alone." He had already replaced all of the knots in some areas where the rug was worn bare; the ends of the knots were still uneven, but

ruled the Middle East, North Africa, and much of southeastern Europe for almost five hundred years. But the original homeland of the Turks was much further east, near the Altai Mountains, where the present borders of Russia, Mongolia, China, and Kazakhstan come together. Turkish-speaking tribes spread out thousands of years ago from that area and eventually occupied much of Central Asia—another name for which is "Turkistan" ("land of the Turks"). They now include such diverse peoples as the Uighurs of northwestern China, the Uzbeks of the large Central Asian republic of Uzbekistan, the Turkmens of Turkmenistan and nearby Iran and Afghanistan, the Azeris of Azerbaijan, and the Osmanlis of Turkey. Over time, the languages, customs, and sense of identity of the various Turkish peoples have diverged somewhat, but in other ways the Turks consider themselves a single people. Although Khaliq regrets that there are few of his fellow Turkmens in America, he feels comfortable in the larger Turkish American community that includes Osmanlis, Uzbeks, and others.

they would all be trimmed to the same short, crisp length when he was finished. "The owners said to me, 'We want this restored completely, whatever it takes.' So I told them, 'That will cost you a lot of money. A *lot* of money.' And they said, 'We don't care, go ahead.' This is a big job, but when I am done this rug will be very beautiful again. And it will last a long, long time."

From Afghanistan to America

Khaliq was born and brought up in the town of Andkhovoi in northwestern Afghanistan. Just a few miles from the border with Turkmenistan, and not far from the Amu Darya River, Andkhovoi is an ethnically mixed town, like most of

Afghanistan. Many people who live there are Turkmens, heirs to a tradition of rug weaving that goes back to their roots as one of the nomadic peoples of ancient Central Asia. Khaliq's family have been rug weavers for many generations. In the normal course of things, Khaliq would still be living in Andkhovoi, working in the rug trade.

Khaliq, however, had the bad luck to grow up in Afghanistan during a very troubled and dangerous time. Much of his childhood was spent in a war zone. Afghanistan had long been ruled by a king, but the monarchy was overthrown in 1973, and in 1978 a pro-Russian Communist government took power. In 1979 the Soviet Union sent troops to defend that government from widespread revolts. After a decade of brutal but fruitless fighting, the Soviets withdrew from Afghanistan, leaving the country to its own resources. Several different rebel groups resumed fighting in different parts of the country, and the Marxist government finally collapsed in 1992. That did not end the fighting, however, and finally in 1995 a fanatical group of Islamic fundamentalists, the Taliban, took over most of the country, with consequences that are with us today.

By then Khaliq and his family had joined the hundreds of thousands of refugees who fled from Afghanistan to escape the wars. The situation for members of ethnic minority groups, such as the Turkmens, had become especially bad. Some Afghans resented the Turkmens in Afghanistan, calling them foreigners and ignorant, lowly sheepherders. The decades of warfare in Afghanistan not only brought the danger of being caught in the

al costume for a Turkmen child, decorated
, coins, beads, and shells.

crossfire of battle but also gave some people an excuse to take advantage of ethnic
differences to expand their own power.
Many Turkmens were persecuted, tor-
tured, or even executed in an Afghan version of "ethnic cleansing." Many left the
country as refugees and now live in
Pakistan or Turkey or in Germany,
England, America, and other countries
in the West. Khaliq's mother and older
brother left for Pakistan in 1988 and made
their way to America; two years later Khaliq
and his younger brother joined them.

A Turkmen in New York

After his family was settled in America,
Khaliq made a trip to Turkey to marry a
young Turkmen woman whose family had
also fled from Afghanistan. They now
have a four-year-old son and are comfortably settled in the richly diverse borough

Khaliq at work

and restorer at the Antique Rug Gallery. He has worked there ever since. Life is good in America for Khaliq and his family, but he regrets one thing: there is no Turkmen community here at all, even in Queens. In fact there are only a handful of Turkmen families in the whole United States.

"I speak Turkmen at home and on the phone with my mother and brothers," he says. "Also on the phone with a few Turkmen friends in different parts of the country. But," he adds with a laugh, "the reason my English is not better is not because I speak Turkmen a lot, but because I speak Persian at work every day." At the rug restoration studio at the Antique Rug Gallery, the workers come from Iran, Pakistan, Afghanistan—all over western Central Asia—and Persian is the one language they all have in common, so that is what they use.

In Turkmenistan, and in Turkmen communities in other nearby countries, many men still ordinarily wear their dis-

of Queens, New York. (Khaliq's mother now lives in Nebraska, where his younger brother is a university student.) As soon as he arrived in America, Khaliq was able, through friends, to get a job as a rug repairer

tinctive ethnic dress—baggy trousers, long shirts, and, most noticeably, big sheepskin hats and long, striped capes. (In 2002 Afghanistan's provisional president, Hamid Karzai, made fashion news when he deliberately chose to dress in a way that combined elements of the traditional dress of many of Afghanistan's peoples, including the Turkmen cape.) I asked Khaliq if he sometimes wore Turkmen clothes in America. "No," he replied, "because there are not enough of us to get together for traditional occasions like weddings. I've never worn Turkmen clothes here." Then he stopped to reconsider. "Actually, I did once, at an exhibition of antique rugs, where I wore traditional clothes and did a demonstration of rug weaving. But that was just for show."

In Khaliq's case, the strongest link to his old homeland is through food. "There are no Turkmen restaurants here, again because there are too few of us," he explains. "But we eat Turkmen food at home every day. That is how we keep our identity." What, I asked, is special about Turkmen food? "Our *nan* bread is different from Pakistani or Iranian *nan;* it is round and soft, and much thicker. And we make rice *pilaf* nomad-style, cooked in one big pot. When my mother comes to visit, she makes a dish that is like a layer cake, with layers of *nan,* lamb, peppers, and onions, baked for a long time. Of course if we were living in a *yurt* [felt tent], we would cook it by burying the pot underneath the campfire. In a house you can't do that, and so it doesn't taste quite as good."

Magic Carpets

Rug weaving is a very ancient craft, because rugs and other woolen textiles have been important to the lives of the nomads of Central Asia since prehistoric times. Thousands of years ago, when people in the more fertile regions of Eurasia were inventing agriculture and settling down in villages to be farmers, the peoples of the grasslands were learning the no less demanding techniques of raising herds of animals. Their lifestyle demanded an exact

A yurt, the round felt tent typical of the Central Asian grasslands

knowledge of local sources of pasture and water in different seasons, expert archery and horsemanship to defend the herds against fierce wild animals and hostile neighbors, and an ability to carry everything they owned on migrations from summer pasture to winter pasture and back again. Women of the nomadic tribes became expert at making many kinds of cloth from the wool that their sheep provided: felt for tents; woven fabrics for clothing; and saddle cloths, storage bags, and rugs from knotted textiles. Just as felt tents provided warm, portable houses on the cold and windy grasslands, rugs provided warm, soft floors for those tents. And while rugs may have been invented from necessity, they became beautiful from the instinctive human tendency to decorate things.

The oldest rug now known was found in a frozen tomb at Pazyryk (pronounced "Pa-zuh-rik"), in southern Siberia, near the Altai Mountains. Dating

to about 500 B.C., it has a beautiful pictorial theme with bands of repeating patterns of horse riders and reindeer. From this we know that all of the essential features of rug weaving were fully developed at least 2,500 years ago; people then were producing rugs with a quality and sophistication that matches those of today. The basic technique has not changed at all. Rugs are made by tying knots of woolen yarn onto warp (lengthwise) threads strung on a loom. Patterns are created by using different colors of yarn for the knots; after every row of knots, the weaver weaves in a weft (crosswise) thread to hold the rug together. The ends of the knots are trimmed to form a smooth, even surface; this is what gives a rug its softness, thickness, and warmth.

The craft of rug weaving had its origins in the daily lives of the nomadic peoples of Central Asia, but rugs eventually became an industry and a business as well as a craft. Rugs were being produced in commercial workshops in Turkey and Persia (Iran) as early as the fourteenth century and were exported along ancient Silk Road routes to places as far away as Europe and China. Eventually rugs were produced in many different countries, but rugs from Central Asia and the Middle East continued to maintain their reputation for fine workmanship and design. Rugs produced commercially for sale or export tended to have more elaborate and complex designs than tribal rugs and sometimes were made of silk rather than wool.

An Ersari Turkmen
dyeing wool for a rug

Rugs and Tribes

From ancient times down to the present, the pastoral nomads of Asia have formed social units called tribes. (The word "tribe" is often used loosely and incorrectly to refer to many different kinds of non-European cultures; here we are using the word with its correct and appropriate meaning.) Tribal society is organized, in effect, from the bottom up. The family is the basic social unit. Families join together as clans, which work cooperatively during migrations and other times of need. Clans in turn come together to form subtribes, and subtribes form tribes. At every level of tribal society, people are united by common beliefs, common language, and mutual needs.

The people of a tribe show who they are through recognizable clothing, jewelry, hats, and other attributes. In Central Asia,

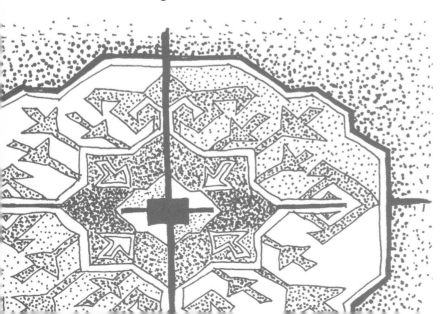

Ersari Turkmen women weaving a rug on a horizontal loom

the rugs they wove in Andkhovoi employed the distinctive Ersari designs. "My mother never needed to use a printed pattern when she wove a rug," says Khaliq. "She knew all of the family patterns by heart, and she just wove freehand. Her rugs always turned out perfectly."

In the Turkmen tradition, the actual weaving of rugs is done by women and girls, as is the spinning of yarn; but men also play a part by raising and shearing sheep, dying the woolen yarn, and handling the sale of finished rugs. "When I was just a child," Khaliq remembers, "I liked to help my mother while she was weaving. I would work on things like binding the side edges of a rug with thread or braiding the fringe at each end." He also learned when he was young the special skills of repairing worn rugs, and that has been his craft ever since. His workshop in New York brings him an endless supply of rugs that need help.

these markers of tribal identity include distinctive patterns of rugs. Every tribe and subtribe has its own patterns, and different ethnic and regional groups also use different kinds of knots. Khaliq's family, like most Turkmens in Afghanistan, belong to the Ersari subtribe, and all of

Khaliq weaving a patch for an antique rug

Saving the Life of an Antique Rug

High-quality antique rugs are works of art, and they can be extremely valuable, with prices for good rugs sometimes in the tens of thousands of dollars. But rugs are also fragile; they can get worn and torn, frayed and stained, and then they need repair or restoration. Khaliq knows all of the different knots that are used by rug makers in different countries and regions, and his workshop is filled with yarns in different weights and thickness and of every possible color. In repairing a rug, he might weave in knots where the originals have worn off, or weave a whole replacement section where the original has worn away completely, or add structural threads where the rug is torn. Ends and edges often need rebinding. But when an antique rug is restored, is it still an antique?

That is where artistic judgment comes in, and where Khaliq's long family background in rug making becomes important. Khaliq understands rugs and loves to work with them. "A fine antique rug is too precious to allow it to wear out," he says. "But if you restore it too much, you can kill its spirit. You wind up just making it into a new rug. What you want to do is stabilize and protect the rug, but not do anything to alter its personality."

Watching Khaliq weave a patch for the badly damaged rug from Boston, his fingers flying as he tied the knots, his razor-sharp knife flicking to cut the thread of each knot before tying the next one, I was struck not only by his concentration, but by the look of quiet pleasure on his face. "I love working on a rug of this quality," he said. "It is very satisfying to take a rug like this, which was so badly damaged, and bring it back to life."

Tamara Katayev
Bukharan Singer

amara Katayev opens the door to her comfortable apartment in Queens, New York, and flashes a smile that lights up the whole hallway. "Hello, I am Tamara," she says in a slightly husky voice. "Please come in." And you know right away: Tamara is a star. It is a quality that every Hollywood producer looks for—a combination of energy, self-confidence, and an intense desire to be liked by everyone. Sitting at her dining room table, chatting over a cup of coffee, it is easy to imagine what a dynamic presence Tamara must be on stage, as she performs the songs and dances of her native Central Asia.

Tamara is proud to continue a musical tradition that goes back hundreds of years to the ancient culture of Bukhara.

Bukhara in Asia

The city of Bukhara was an important oasis and trading center on the Silk Road. The city and the surrounding region fell under the rule of one empire after another at different times during its long history, but Bukhara was always a major contributor to the culture and commerce of Central Asia.

The Jewish community of Bukhara dates back to at least the early fifteenth

ve: Tamara's
her (far left)
friends, 1936.
t: Tamara
cing

century and probably is much older than that. Some members of the community were merchants and bankers engaged in the Silk Road trade, including the trade in rugs from nearby cities and tribal areas. Many Jews were skilled workers involved in leather, metal, and other craft occupations. In the nineteenth century they were known especially as expert weavers and dyers who produced the colorful, high-quality silk cloth for which the region became famous. Some Bukharan Jews also became musicians, whose talents were sought not just within the Jewish community, but also by other groups in the multicultural environment of Central Asia. Tamara comes from a family of traditional musicians, and her earliest memories are of her parents playing instruments, singing, and dancing. Now, in New York City, Tamara performs the same songs and dances that she learned from her parents.

Bukharan musicians with *doire* frame-drums, c. 1880

Bukhara in Queens

Tamara and her family belong to a large Bukharan Jewish community in Queens, New York. When the Soviet Union destabilized in 1989, many members of the Jewish communities of Bukhara, Samarkand, Tashkent, and other Central Asian cities were worried. As the former Soviet Republics in the region moved toward independence (they are now Uzbekistan, Kazakhstan, Tadjikistan, Turkmenistan, and Kyrgyzstan), it was not clear that their new governments would be able to maintain order. "It is not so easy to be Jewish in such a place," says Tamara. "We were not sure that we would be safe. It seemed that it would be best for us to leave." Many members of the community went to Europe and then on to Israel; several thousand chose to come to America instead.

Tamara, her husband, and their four children, along with her mother and other relatives, left Tashkent for Europe. After living for a while in Austria and Italy, they came to America in 1990. Like so many other New York immigrant families, Tamara and her family and friends are pleased and proud to be Americans, but they are also careful to preserve as much of their traditional culture as possible. In the attractive, middle-class Queens neighborhoods of Rego Park, Kew Gardens, and Forest Hills, they have found some of the atmosphere of their old homeland. Many of the shop signs are in Russian or Uzbek, local restaurants serve delicious Central Asian food, and synagogues and Jewish community organizations help knit the community together. Best of all, from Tamara's point of view, three theaters and numerous restaurants and nightclubs offer a steady diet of traditional Bukharan Jewish music and dance. There is never a shortage of places for Tamara to perform.

A Family Tradition

"My life has always been filled with music," says Tamara. Her mother and father were both well-known performers whose talents were officially recognized by the government of the Soviet Union. Her mother's father was Gavriel ben Aharon Mullokandov, the greatest Bukharan musician of the twentieth century, a man who was famous throughout Central Asia.

They lived in the ancient city of Samarkand, rich in traditions of the Silk Road. Tamara loved the atmosphere of the performing arts that she grew up with at home, and she learned to sing and dance almost as soon as she could talk and walk.

"My two sisters and my brother also learned music, of course," Tamara continues, "but when they grew up they followed other professions. But for me, music was the center of my life. I couldn't imagine doing anything else, and I was proud to follow in my parents' footsteps." She made her professional debut on stage at the age of ten and performed all during her teenage years. Then she joined a group called Gulshan that performed regularly on Samarkand radio and television stations and had a very multicultural audience. As one of the group's soloists, Tamara sang in Afghani (Pashtun), Turkish, Persian, Uzbek, Arabic, and Russian.

"But then I got married and moved with my husband to Tashkent." (Like Samarkand, Tashkent is in what is now the independent country of Uzbekistan). "We started a family, and I cut back on my performance schedule in order to stay home and take care of the children." Like

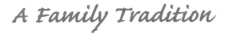

Tamara singing

Tamara's father, 1937, in costume as the emir of Bukhara (photo printed from a broken glass negative)

her own mother, Tamara had three daughters and a son. And she made sure that all of them learned to sing and dance.

When Tamara's family came to America in 1990 and joined the growing Bukharan community in New York, she was already well known as a singer and dancer, and she quickly began to get invitations to join various groups of performers. In recent years she has been a soloist with a group called Maqam, led by the Bukharan poet and musician Ilyas Malayev. She has also been a featured performer for several years at the International Jewish Folk Life Festival of Long Island, with another group called Mazaltov (which means "good luck"), and has toured with these and other groups throughout America, Europe, and Israel. When she performs, wearing a traditional costume glittering with gold thread and accompanying her singing and dancing with complicated rhythms played on a frame-drum, she feels as if she is back in Central Asia again.

What Is Bukharan Music?

Bukharan traditional music, called *shash-maqam* (pronounced "shash-mak-kam"), is a unique blend of Tadjik (Persian), Uzbek (Turkish), and Middle Eastern (Arab and Jewish) elements. This ability to absorb and reflect influences from several cultures made Bukharan Jewish music popular in all communities in its Central Asian homeland, and it continues to evolve today, both in Asia and New York. Much of the music is very rhythmical, designed for dancing. The instruments of an ensemble vary, but a large frame-drum called a *doire* (or *doura*), which looks like a very big tambourine without the metal jingles around the edge, is always included. Other instruments likely to be used are the *tar* and the *tanbur*, long-necked, plucked stringed instruments in the lute family (see the chapter in this book on Peter Kyvelos, the oud maker) and the *gidjak*, a long-necked bowed instrument in the violin family.

The dances performed to this music are both graceful and exciting. After the orchestra has played a brief introductory passage, Tamara rises from where she has been sitting with the musicians and steps forward, her feet beginning to move in rapid, complicated patterns. The steps carry her forward and backward or in

Tamara and the Ensemble Maqam at the Smithsonian Folklife Festival's New York City program in 2001

whirling turns, but her body is held upright and rather still, giving even fast dances an air of dignity. She holds her arms above her head as she turns, or lowers her arms to make expressive movements with her hands at shoulder level; in some dances she continues to play her *doire* frame-drum. The movements of the brightly costumed dancers and the intensity of the strongly rhythmic music seem to cast a kind of hypnotic spell over the people in the audience.

In the twentieth century more instruments gradually began to be used by Bukharan musicians, including the violin, mandolin, accordion, clarinet, and saxophone. With these instruments came new musical influences, and some Bukharan music is strongly influenced by the klezmer music of the Eastern European and Russian Jewish communities (and klezmer itself is a mixture of European, Middle Eastern, and Gypsy music).

Bukharan performer Feruza Yagudayeva, a member of the Ensemble Maqam, at the Smithsonian Folklife Festival

Tamara and the other musicians she performs with believe that it is important to preserve the oldest and most traditional styles of music, but they also think it is good that their music is still alive and changing as it encounters other kinds of music and absorbs new influences. Many of the musicians Tamara works with are also poets and songwriters, and the new music that they produce also helps to keep their tradition fresh and alive. Tamara herself has written some folk songs, including this one, which expresses the fears and worries of a young woman who is about to be married, in a culture where marriages are still more likely to be set up by matchmakers than to be love matches of the young people themselves:

A Folk-Song Written by Tamara Katayev

I Don't Want to Get Married

I don't want to get married.
I want to stay with my mother in her
*   house.*
At my mother's house there's a pen and
*   paper,*
But at my husband's house there is anger
*   and fights.*
When I'm with my mother I learn
More and more new skills,
But when I'm with my husband
Everything becomes bitter.
My mother has the best food,
Such as warm tandur bread and figs,
But with my husband there's no freedom.
My mother has many sweets,
But at my husband's I have to
Give birth and raise
*   his children.*

Bukhara: A Turbulent History

The city of Bukhara, and the surrounding province of the same name, were conquered by Alexander the Great in 334 B.C., the first of many times that Bukhara became part of a larger empire. In the seventh century the people of Bukhara converted to Islam, and the region became a province of the great Abbassid Empire ruled from Baghdad. In the thirteenth century, Bukhara was conquered by Genghiz Khan and brought under the control of the vast Mongol Empire. A century later, it was incorporated into the Mongol-Turkish empire of Timur Leng (Tamerlane), who turned the Silk Road oasis town of Samarkand, not far from Bukhara, into a wealthy and splendid capital city. With the death of Timur Leng in 1405, his

A *madraseh* (Islamic school) in Bukhara, c. 1960

empire broke up, and Bukhara became an independent kingdom at that time. Its rulers were known first as khans, later as emirs. The Emirate of Bukhara fell under the domination of Russia in 1868 and was incorporated into the Soviet Union in 1925 as part of the Uzbek Soviet

Republic. Since 1989, with the breakup of the Soviet Union, the Uzbek Soviet Republic in turn became the independent nation of Uzbekistan. This long, colorful, and rather violent history has given Bukhara an interesting culture that is a mixture of many different influences.

Will the Tradition Survive?

In the New York Bukharan Jewish community, many people have tried consciously to preserve as much of the community's traditional culture as possible. As Ilyas Malayev has said, "If a nation can preserve its musical heritage, and thereby its culture, then such a nation is forever alive." But in spite of these efforts, Tamara is worried that already the tradition of Bukharan music in New York is starting to fade. She notices, for example, that at the kinds of family events where one might expect people to want traditional music, other influences are more and more evident. When asked if she often sang at weddings and bar mitzvahs, she replied, with a flash of annoyance, "I don't like to accept such invitations. Always at weddings and bar mitzvahs, people ask me to sing Western songs that I don't know, or that I don't like to sing. I very much pre-

fer to perform on stage, where we can play the kind of music that we want."

The audiences who cheer her performances on stage are enthusiastic, but very few of the people in those audiences are under thirty years old. This worries Tamara a great deal. "The young people of the community don't care about traditional music, either to listen or to perform. They all want to be like Michael Jackson," she says, sadly. None of her own children have become professional performers. "Of course in America there are many more career choices for them, so I can't complain if they don't want to make their livings on stage. At least when we get together as a family, we always make music together."

Tamara's expression brightens as she shows pictures of her youngest daughter dancing. Svetlana, in her late teens, is an expert singer and dancer. Even though she doesn't plan a professional career in

The Ensemble Maqam taking a bow after a performance

music, she often performs with youth groups, including a recent concert at the United Nations. And the next generation of Tamara's family is continuing the family tradition, too, especially a four-year-old granddaughter who lives with her family in Florida. "She is very talented, a very good dancer, and she learns fast," boasts the proud grandmother. "She always asks, 'When is Grandma Tamara going to come to teach me a new song?'"

As long as there are such grandmothers and such grandchildren, Tamara's traditional music will continue to live.

Najmieh Batmanglij
Iranian American Cook

Foods were among the most important goods that traveled along the Silk Road: spices, of course, but also fruits, vegetables, grains, and methods of cooking. Archeologists have found pieces of Middle Eastern bread, preserved in the dry climate of northern China, dating back to the seventh century A.D.

The country now called Iran is at the core of what was once the huge Persian Empire. Strong military leaders like King Darius I, or "Darius the Great," who took power in 522 B.C., pushed the borders of the empire west to Greece and east to the Indus River. Artistic and literary influences from the conquered cultures found a home in Persia. Such a vast empire couldn't be defended forever, and succeeding waves of conquests from the Greeks, Arabs, Mongols, and Turks swept over Persia, adding new cultural influences each time. This continual blending of cultures made for a rich combination of East and West, and the result is certainly reflected in Persian cooking.

Persian men cooking at a picnic. Detail f
a sixteenth-century watercolor with g

A woman in Eastern Iran making bread

Many foods native to Persia traveled both east and west, and foods from other lands found a home there as well. Almonds, dates, pomegranates, mint, coriander, saffron, and caraway are all said to have originated in Persia. On the other hand, some foods found in most Iranian homes today came to the area very late. Tea, for instance, did not arrive until 1868, by way of England and India. Today, most Iranian hostesses (even in America, as you will find out) serve tea from large metal samovars (large containers that keep water hot) to their guests.

In Najmieh's Kitchen

Najmieh Batmanglij loves everything about food. As soon as you walk into the large kitchen at the back of her Washington, D.C., home, you can tell. Wonderful spicy aromas welcome you. Strings of garlic and hot peppers join beautiful Iranian pottery and metal bowls, tablecloths, and other decorations all around the room. The long butcher-block counter and the appliances (stove, oven, refrigerator) are all arranged within easy reach of the cook.

But before Najmieh begins cooking for her guests, she sits them down at a round table and serves tea in tiny glass cups from a steaming samovar, and sweets in several small bowls. Failing to serve these goodies would be impolite for an Iranian American hostess, and refusing them would be very bad form for a guest.

Najmieh sits down with her guests to chat. She is a warm and cheerful person who laughs often. Her eyes sparkle when she talks about anything to do with food. You would never guess the sorrow she has been through, forced to leave her beloved native Iran and her family and start a new life in America. But the story comes out as she talks about food.

Najmieh keeps water hot for tea in a large samovar.

A Cook Is Born

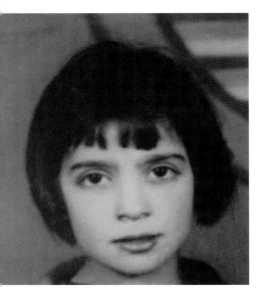

Najmieh at age seven

Najmieh Batmanglij grew up in a big family full of good cooks and good food. Some of her earliest and fondest memories are of the times women would gather at her house to make noodles or when her family would gather for New Year's ceremony (the first day of spring in Iran).

As a little girl, she always watched her mother and aunts cooking and wanted to be a cook herself. But her mother told her, "I never had a chance to get a university education, but you do. You will have plenty of opportunities to cook later." When she was eighteen, she left Iran for the first time to go to college in America.

Cooking Up an Education

While in college in Connecticut, Najmieh lived in a "big, old house" with four other students. "I did all the cooking and wrote home whenever I couldn't get a Persian recipe right. I resorted to cookbooks to make pizza, pasta, or Chinese food." To her delight, everyone liked her cooking, especially the Persian dishes.

After college, she stayed in America and received her master's degree. In 1975, she returned to Iran. "I handed my degree to my mother so she'd let me into the kitchen!" Although she started working a full-time job as well as another part-time job, she spent every free moment learning how to cook traditional Persian food from her mother. She also learned how to pick the freshest fruits and vegetables at the markets, how to combine herbs and spices, and how to make home remedies with food.

Najmieh makes the tricky job of seeding a pomegranate look easy. First, she peels a section to expose the seeds. Then, she whacks it with a wooden spoon to loosen the seeds and removes them with her fingers. The tangy-sweet seeds are used in salads or desserts.

Memories of Noodle-Making Day

By Najmieh Batmanglij, from *Silk Road Cooking: A Vegetarian Journey*

The origin of noodles, or pasta, is shrouded in history, but there is some evidence that the Persians invented them, and that travelers spread them east and west. The Chinese were cooking noodle dishes as early as the Han Dynasty, which ended in 220 A.D. It is speculated that Arabs had brought noodles to Italy by the ninth century A.D., which means that the old story of Marco Polo introducing them to Italy is not true at all. Here is Najmieh's own childhood memory of making noodles.

Exploring Silk Road culinary links brings back many scenes from my Persian childhood in Iran. On certain school half days, when I arrived home early in the afternoon, I would hear distant echoes of a *setar* and my mother's voice singing. The sweet, sad tones drew me to the brightest room in our house, where, sitting on the Persian carpet striped with light and color from the sunshine that seeped through bamboo shades, I found my mother and four or five old ladies, all distant relatives. From the crisply ironed white cotton cloths being spread over the carpet and the captivating aroma of fresh dough, I knew it was noodle-making day. "Come on in," said the old ladies, tearing off a piece of dough for me to play with. They were kneading dough and rolling it into rectangles on large wooden boards. When they had rolled it thin, they folded each sheet twice; then, with one hand as a guide and working with fast, confident strokes, they used sharp knives to cut their dough sheets into quarter-inch strips. The room would fall silent as they concentrated on the task, joyfully competing to see who could cut the most even strips in the shortest time.

Every so often, as if reminded by something, my mother would stop cutting, put down her knife, and take up singing her poem from where she had left off. Everyone would stop working, some still kneading the dough, some with finished strips in hand. All would lean back from their work and join in the refrain. Just as quickly as it had started, the singing would stop.

Our housekeeper Naneh would bring in tea, there would be some gossip, a few new jokes, lots of laughing. Then, as if on cue, everyone would go back to work.

One of the old ladies would give me some strands of the

fresh noodles to arrange, carefully separated for drying, on the floured cotton sheets. I found myself as delighted by the cheerful ceremony of preparation as by the reward for the work.

The next day, convivial crowds of relatives would come to our house for a glorious lunch of noodle soup garnished with fried garlic, onion, mint, and sun-dried yogurt.

Such happy memories inspired me years later, when I turned to a more serious study of cookery. You can find the noodle soup recipe and its headnote on page 40 in my book *A Taste of Persia*.

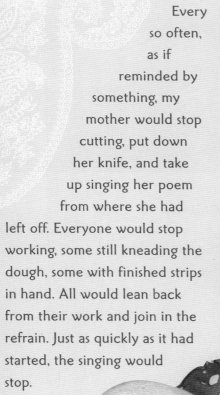

rl selling melons
 her family at a
ket in
ekistan, one of
countries Najmieh
ed on her trip
g the Silk Road

Everyone around the world loves cookies. Here is a recipe that Najmieh has adapted from Persia and other Silk Road countries. It is easy for kids to make, but (of course) consult an adult when using the oven.

East-West Almond Cookies

Makes: 15 cookies
Preparation time: 15 minutes
Cooking time: 8–10 minutes

Ingredients:

- 1 cup blanched almonds
- 1 cup granulated sugar
- 1/2 cup corn oil
- 5 egg whites lightly beaten
- 1 cup all-purpose flour, sifted
- 1 teaspoon ground cardamom
- 2 tablespoons rose water (special for cooking)

Decoration:

- 2 tablespoons unsalted ground pistachios or almond slices
- 2 tablespoons organic rose petals

These cookies are made all along the Silk Road from Italy to China.

A plate of almond cookies waiting to be tasted. A metal mortar and pestle are at the left corner of the picture

Procedure:

1. Preheat the oven to 425°F. Grease a cookie sheet.
2. Finely grind the almonds in a food processor and set aside.
3. Beat the sugar and oil in a mixing bowl until you have a soft paste.
4. Add the egg white and beat for 20 seconds. Fold in the flour, almonds, cardamom, and rose water and gently blend for 20 seconds, until you have a smooth batter.
5. Scoop out a full teaspoon of the batter and place it on the greased cookie sheet. Continue to fill up the cookie sheet, leaving $2\frac{1}{2}$ inches between each cookie for expansion. Decorate each cookie with the pistachios and rose petal.
6. Place the cookie sheet in the center of the oven and bake for 8–10 minutes, or until the edges of the cookies are golden.
7. Take the cookie sheet out of the oven and immediately remove the cookies, using a spatula to lift the cookies from the sheet. Do this while the cookies are still hot; they won't come off easily once cool.

Home Cooking

"I led a thoroughly modern life, yet I was interested in traditional cooking and the uses of herbs. This fascinated many of the older generation of family and friends. One of my aunts, for example, was an excellent pastry chef who made the best baklava in Tehran. Once she saw that I would come back from work and put on my apron, she agreed to teach me how she did it. She said she had not shown anyone how to do this ever before."

In the next four years, Najmieh learned all she could about cooking from family and friends, jotting down recipes in a notebook. During this time, she also met her husband, and her cooking skills won his heart. "We had known each other for a few weeks, and he came back from duck hunting with two mallards. He asked if I could cook them. I had never cooked wild game before, but my mother came to my rescue, and the duck with pomegranate sauce was a great success!"

French Cooking

In 1979, a revolution broke out in Iran. Although young people like Najmieh at first thought the revolution would be a good thing, it quickly turned bad. She and other young people made the hard decision to leave their country and start a new life somewhere else. Najmieh left her family and went to the south of France on a cold December day in 1980. "That was the saddest day of my life."

Her husband was not able to leave Iran at that time, so she was alone, pregnant with her first son, and miserable. She could speak only a little French. Food helped build a bridge between her and the local folks in the small coastal town she was staying in. She signed up for a cooking class.

"I quickly realized that as much as I was interested in learning from the French chefs, they wanted to learn about Persian food from me. They were thirsty for new ideas and new tastes."

She made friends with many people in the community, and her language skills improved rapidly as she started translating Persian recipes into French. This work eventually became her first cookbook, *Ma Cuisine d'Iran* (my Iranian cuisine), published in 1984.

Coming to America

In 1983, Najmieh and her husband decided to emigrate to America. She had another son soon after coming to the United States. She began to write another cookbook in English. *Food of Life: Ancient Persian and Modern Iranian Cooking and Ceremonies* was published in 1986. Since then, she has published five more cookbooks. She also teaches cooking in her home and travels around giving lectures on food. Her cooking has impressed such groups as the Academy of Sciences, the Culinary Institute of America, the Smithsonian, and the Faculty Club at Harvard University.

Her latest book is a vegetarian cookbook with recipes from Iran and other Silk Road countries from Italy to China. To research this cookbook, she traveled to each country, talked to cooks, and sampled many different types of food. Like the early travelers along the Silk Road, Najmieh's writings on the foods she discovered will help bring an important part of these cultures to an appreciative audience of cooks and families.

"I have not spent a day when some aspect of cooking has not been a part of my life," she says. She feels that the most enjoyable type of cooking is gathering friends and family around to help. Her sons, who are now teenagers, often join in.

Ancient Tradition in Modern Life

Najmieh's cooking brings very old Persian traditions together with up-to-date technology and tastes. To grind some herbs, she uses a mortar and pestle, but for many ingredients, she uses her food processor. Americans today are interested in trying new types of foods, and Persian food fits right into this adventurous spirit. Ingredients that used to be hard to find, such as pomegranate paste, are now available in Middle Eastern markets in many parts of the United States, and also can be ordered from the Internet.

In Iran, food is not only something you eat. It is at the center of family life, social occasions, and holidays. It can also be used as medicine. Traditional Persian food is carefully balanced between sweet and sour, hot and cold. Najmieh explains

Najmieh shopping for fresh produce at the Fresh Farms Market, Dupont Circle, Washington, D.C.

that "hot and cold" in Persian cooking does not mean temperature. Instead, different foods have different characteristics. Dates and chocolate are considered hot (*garmi* in Persian) and thicken the blood. Watermelon and grapefruit juice are cold (*sardi*) foods that dilute the blood.

People can have hot or cold natures. Najmieh's son, for instance, has a hot nature, and eating too much chocolate or dates makes him feel sick. To restore his balance, she gives him some juice from a "cold" fruit.

Najmieh and her family enjoy many different holidays and celebrations. Many traditional Persian celebrations follow the seasons, including New Year's (Nowruz), Winter Feast (Shab-e yalda) and Autumn Festival (Jashn-e mehregan). But one of the Batmanglij family's favorite celebrations is the American holiday of Thanksgiving, which falls near the birthday of one of Najmieh's sons. Najmieh's husband is in charge of cooking the turkey. Last year, family and friends enjoyed his Chinese-style Szechuan turkey so much that it might become a new tradition.

Now there's a Silk Road story for you.

il from a painting in an Iranian
uscript from around 1570

կայ եւ եկեղեցյո

ե թերեկրոյէ ճշմ

արիա ։

Ո ապատատան

թենյանեատցին

La Verne Magarian
Armenian American
Calligrapher and Paper Artist

Of all the people portrayed in this book, La Verne J. Magarian is the furthest removed from her Silk Road heritage. Her grandparents, who were Armenian, came to America from present-day Turkey, escaping religious and political persecution that led to the deaths of many others. She grew up well aware of her Armenian heritage, yet it was not until much later in life that she became interested in studying an important ancient Armenian art: the creation of beautiful illuminated manuscript pages.

Since her house in Potomac, Maryland, is soon to be renovated, she brings her work and her family treasures in several big portfolios and boxes, a kind of movable tribute to her life and art. Unfolding samples of her grandmother's tatted lace doilies, an exquisitely woven Armenian textile, a small Bible printed in Armenian, and family photos of her grandparents' immaculate home and her

La Verne's great uncle's tailor shop in Fresno, California

La Verne's maternal grandparents

great-uncle's tailor shop, alongside her own artwork, La Verne's face shows both pride and sadness. She misses her family, most of whom have passed away, but she feels that her current work brings her closer to them in spirit.

There are also stacks of books on Armenian history, art, and cooking. They are well-worn with lots of notes in the margins. Leafing through these, you learn some basic information about Armenian culture through the ages, and can see why La Verne is so interested in recapturing some of her own heritage.

Armenian History

Armenia today is a small country that gained its independence from the former Soviet Union in 1991. But in ancient times, around the first century B.C. under Tigranes the Great, Armenia was a large empire that stretched from the Caspian Sea to the Mediterranean Sea, including parts of Georgia and Syria. Because of its strategic location for commerce and the launch of military campaigns, it was conquered by a succession of other powerful empires: the Romans, Persians, Byzantines, Arabs, Mongols, and Ottomans.

The Armenian people, overtaken and often divided by such fluctuations in rulership, could easily have been absorbed into other cultures. One significant fact helped them keep their distinctiveness. In the first century A.D., two of Jesus's apostles came to preach in Armenia and converted many people to Christianity. At first, Armenian Christians were persecuted, but finally the king of Armenia, Tiridates, was converted himself. Armenia became the first nation to proclaim Christianity its official religion. Over the years, surrounded and conquered by a succession of non-Christian nations, the Armenians were often persecuted and driven from their homes, resulting in the growth of Armenian communities in many lands around the world.

Armenian Art, Culture, and Language: The Book

Christianity had a profound effect on Armenian art, culture, and language. For one thing, the Bible had to be translated into Armenian from Greek. So an alphabet had to be invented for the Armenian language, a task completed by scholar Mesrob Mashtots in 406 A.D. The Bible, and books in general, took on great importance in Armenian culture over the years. Bibles were illustrated with beautiful script and miniature paintings with gold (called "illumination") and became treasured works of art.

But even plain Bibles and nonreligious books are valuable parts of Armenian life to this day. Books in Armenian symbolize that distinct language and the

Fourteenth-century illustration of a calligrapher at work. Below: the Armenian alphabet, with corresponding letters from the Western alphabet.

 Բ Գ Դ Ե Զ Է Ը Թ Ժ Ի Լ Խ Ծ Կ Հ Ձ Ղ Ճ Մ Յ Ն Շ Ո Չ Պ Ջ Ռ Ս Վ Տ Ր Ց Ւ Փ Ք Օ Ֆ

բ գ դ ե զ է ը թ ժ ի լ խ ծ կ հ ձ ղ ճ մ յ ն շ ո չ պ ջ ռ ս վ տ ր ց ւ փ ք օ ֆ

b g d e z ē ə t' ž i l x c k h j ł č m y n š o č' p ǰ r̄ s v t r c' w p' k' aw f

La Verne's father's aunt, whom she called Auntie Armorel, in traditional Armenian dress for a special occasion

La Verne and her sister Patricia (nicknamed "Che-She") in their grandmother's garden

importance of learning to read. Small Bibles and other books are easy to carry, and when many Armenians were forced to move from their homes in the face of wars and persecution, books were always among the objects they took with them.

Armenians in America

La Verne thinks her grandparents came to America around 1900. Many Armenians came to America, especially after 1915, when the Turkish government sought to get rid of Armenians living in their country. It is estimated that more than a million and a half Armenians were killed during this period

In America, Armenians—who even during Silk Road days thrived as merchants and artisans—became prosperous, many owning their own businesses. Today, they are typically very close-knit and family-oriented.

Armenian/American

La Verne's grandparents settled in Fresno, California, one of the largest Armenian American communities in America. She remembers as a young child being confused about whether she was Armenian or American. "I was surrounded by Armenian food, the Armenian language, and Armenian ways of doing things. Both words started with a capital *A* and ended with *n,* and they both had eight letters!"

Of course, she was both. Her parents moved to Vallejo, California, where there were only a handful of Armenian families. Armenian was spoken only occasionally, and La Verne and her sister never mastered the Armenian language. They did visit her maternal grandparents, aunt, and uncle in Fresno often, where Armenian was spoken. She remembers that her grandmother grew her own special Armenian cucumbers (called *guta*) and other fresh herbs and vegetables that she used in cooking traditional foods. "She always had a pot of soup cooking on the stove."

Bread was baked at home or bought at one of the many Armenian bakeries in Fresno. Like much of Armenian culture, food was influenced by Armenia's location in the Middle East: flatbreads, shish-kabobs, olives, and rice dishes. La Verne still cooks some of these foods herself.

La Verne's Work: Carrying on the Spirit of Tradition

La Verne's adult life took her far from California and her Armenian heritage. She worked in entomology with her former husband, who was an expert on certain types of beetles (she even has a beetle named after her). She worked for the large company IBM. But in the 1980s she found her true calling, which brought her back to the Armenian love of letters, books, and artistry.

She began studying calligraphy, the art of lettering, in 1986. She also took courses in decorative paper and book making. Her skill increased, and in 1993 she became involved in a very special project. "Because I was Armenian and I did calligraphy and related arts, I received a call that lead me to the Pierpont Morgan Library in New York City. They needed a calligrapher to write Armenian script for an exhibit on illuminated medieval manuscripts."

La Verne was intrigued by the project, but knew she needed to do a lot of work before she could carry out the assignment. "I didn't know the Armenian language or Armenian script, although I

An Armenian
illuminated
manuscript
from the 1994
exhibition at
the Pierpont
Morgan Library

"Learning calligraphy is like a funnel. You start out at the narrow end, wanting to write beautiful letters. Then once you start, you realize that the giant world of calligraphy keeps expanding, the way a funnel flares out. If you want to, you can always keep expanding, keep learning. No one person can ever know everything about calligraphy and its related arts."
—La Verne Magarian

La Verne showing Mary Elinor Francis, age ten, some practice strokes

First, special paper is carefully cut to size.

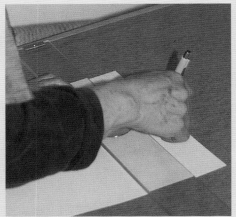

Pencil marks keep the lines of calligraphy even.

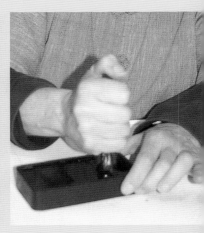

A dry ink stick is ground on a stone slab with water to create the liquid ink.

Directional Strokes	Preliminary Calligraphic Strokes made with a felt-tip pen

Try it yourself! La Verne created these practice strokes for beginners using a felt-tip pen. Follow the directions, but remember, it takes patience.

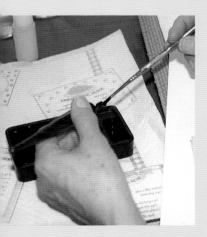

...e new ink is loaded onto the ...ck of the pen's nib, or point.

The end of a brush steadies the pen and careful strokes are made.

A good way to practice is with two pencils held together with a rubber band.

LaVerne at work

each character was made: the stroke, the width, thickness, slant, and spacing. Then I started practicing."

The process took a lot of hard work and much more research. "I went to the Smithsonian's Freer Gallery and looked at thousand-year-old manuscripts. I was looking for just the right red color for the column lines. I had to decide what type of paper to use and figure out how to draw lines as they did in medieval times. It was both scholarly and creative at the same time." By the time the project was finished, she had produced five pieces for the exhibition.

The exhibit project didn't require any illustration, or illumination, but La Verne became so interested in the old manuscripts that she created a modern version of an illuminated manuscript inspired by what she has studied in the medieval illuminated Armenian Gospels. The result is a beautiful, delicate work of art, which she

was surrounded by it in my grandmother's house when I was a child. I went to the Library of Congress and pored through books and selected the best examples of Armenian calligraphy. I analyzed how

had framed and reproduced into note-cards, bookmarks, and the cover of a blank book. "I worked morning to night, seven days a week, and looked forward to getting up in the morning to begin again." It took La Verne nine months to do the exhibition pieces and her own illuminated piece.

Since then, her work has appeared in juried exhibits and she has served as an artist-in-residence at the Washington National Cathedral. Her portfolio includes examples of other kinds of calligraphy, lovely handmade books bound in silk, and "paste papers" (papers often seen on the inside cover of well-made books) in swirling blues, greens, purples, and pinks.

What does she like best about doing her art? "The mystery. I always get the initial feeling, thinking, 'How can I do this?' Then looking back after the process is over and thinking, 'I did that? Could I do it again?'"

Seeing La Verne J. Magarian's work, and learning about her dedication and persistence, you can almost imagine some distant Armenian relative bending over a medieval illuminated manuscript, patient and inspired, creating a treasure that will endure through the ages.

Peter Kyvelos
Greek American Oud Maker

nique Strings is a narrow, cluttered shop in Belmont, a suburb of Boston, Massachusetts. The first thing you notice when you step through the door is a rich, pleasant smell of wood shavings, glue, and varnish. The second thing is the dozens of violins, cellos, guitars, and other less familiar stringed instruments stacked up on shelves all around the shop walls. And then your attention turns to Peter Kyvelos coming up from the back of the shop, a big bear of a man with a warm, friendly smile and a bushy walrus mustache. Although he is meeting you for the first time, he greets you like an old friend. Peter has owned and operated this shop for thirty years, and it obviously fits him as comfortably as an old shoe. If you have a stringed instrument that needs to be repaired, or, even more, if you want to buy an oud from the finest oud maker in America, you have come to the right place. If you want to find out all about ouds and the people who play them, this is the right place too.

What Is an Oud?

The word *oud* comes from the Arabic word *al'ūd*, which means "wood." So the basic meaning of *oud* is "a musical instrument made of wood." Now try saying *al'ūd* over and over again a few times. Soon you might be saying something that sounds like "a lute"—and that is exactly what an oud is. The English word "lute" is simply a changed pronunciation of the original Arabic word (with a couple of steps in between, for example the Provençal (old southern French) word *laud*, and Old French *lut*). Both the instrument and its name entered Europe from Arabic-speaking North Africa via Spain and southern France and then spread northward to Holland, Germany, England, and elsewhere. This happened at least ten or twelve centuries ago. By the fifteenth century, the lute was extremely popular all over Europe, and a great many songs

Haig Manoukian, oud player with the Mesqouda Judeo-Arabic Ensemble, performing at the Smithsonian Folklife Festival's New York City program in 2001

A nineteenth-century Tibetan thangka painting showing the guardian deity Dhritarashtra playing a *pipa*

were written to be played on it or to be sung to a lute accompaniment. Later, other stronger-voiced stringed instruments, especially the piano and the guitar, became more popular than the lute; but the lute is still played today, especially as an instrument in orchestras that specialize in Renaissance and Baroque music.

While the oud was spreading across Europe a thousand years ago, it was also spreading eastward. In fact, what are known as instruments in the lute family are found throughout Europe, North Africa, the Middle East, and all across Asia. The members of this family of musical instruments are all of the same basic type, with several strings, a neck (which might be long, short, or medium in length) with tuning pegs for the strings, and a body shaped like a pear sliced in half. Lutes—ouds—have changed in many ways as they have traveled from culture to culture and country to country, and they are now called by dozens of different

An oud player takes the front seat on this eighth-century Chinese ceramic sculpture (detail).

names, in many different languages. But in a sense they are all basically the same.

Historians of music think that the oldest ancestor of the oud had a very long neck and a small body. Instruments like that were found in the Middle East and in Egypt as much as four thousand years ago, and similar ones are still widely used in Central Asia. One example is the *tar* used in Bukharan music (see the chapter on Tamara Katayev in this book). Gradually, as instrument makers found ways to improve construction techniques, oud-type instruments were made with bigger, louder bodies and with shorter necks that carried more strings. The basic oud was known about two thousand years ago, and instruments of essentially modern type date from about 800 A.D. It has been the most important instrument in Middle Eastern music ever since.

Because the oud is so widespread in the Middle East, it came to America with many different groups of immigrants in the late nineteenth and early twentieth centuries. Greeks, Armenians, Syrians, Lebanese, Egyptians, and many other people from the eastern Mediterranean region came to America, bringing the music of their native lands in their hearts, and in their hands, the musical instruments to play it.

A Greek American Childhood

Peter's father was born in Greece, near the ancient city of Sparta, and came to America as a young man. Peter's mother was born in America, but her parents were Greek. In a typical immigrant success story, soon after he arrived in America, Peter's father started a small business, making and selling handmade candy. His product was good and his prices were right, and soon he built his business up into a big, successful shop on Long Island, near New York City. But after a few years, the stock market crash of 1929 and the depression of the 1930s wiped out his business, and he had to start over. He moved to the central Massachusetts town of Fitchburg and took a job in a factory there. That's where Peter was born and raised.

Fitchburg was an old industrial city, home to immigrants from many different countries. There were large Greek and Armenian communities, but Peter's friends were a very diverse group. He remembers childhood not as an immigrant experience, but as an American one—dominated by school, but with plenty of time for baseball, fishing, bicycle rides, and other ways of having fun. Perhaps what distinguished Peter most from his friends was that he was always making things.

"There was good clay in the banks of the river that ran through town," he remembers, "and I liked to make little sculptures out of the clay, and bake them in a fire. And I loved to do woodcarving; I was always whittling things and giving them away to my friends." His father had a well-equipped workbench at home, and he encouraged Peter to develop his skill

Haig Manoukian playing an oud, and Joshua Levitt playing a *nai* (a type of flute)

with tools. Soon people were asking Peter for help when something needed fixing. When he was about thirteen years old, he discovered that his gift for making things could also be a way of making money.

"I loved to fish, but the trout flies I could buy in Fitchburg weren't very good. I figured I could do better, so I started tying my own. One day I took a dozen of my flies to the local auto parts/fishing tackle store and asked the owner if he thought he could sell them. I went back a few days later, and he had sold them all at thirty-five cents each—good money for those days. He told me to get working, because he could sell as many as I could make."

Most of the money he made from his fly-tying business went to support his other great passion beside fishing—music. Music had been a part of his life since he was a baby, and he couldn't imagine living without it.

Peter's early memories of music come not only from the weddings, christenings, and other family celebrations in the local Greek community, but especially from his father's love of music. "My father played the violin," he explains. "He really wasn't that good at it—not good enough to be a professional, that's for sure. But he would practice at home, playing along with his old 78 rpm records of Greek folk music

A wall of tools above Peter's workbench

and dance music. We had a hand-cranked phonograph, and stacks and stacks of records. That was the music of my childhood."

Peter's experience with music taught him an important lesson: music can bring people together. "The music I grew up with was the music of Greek communities from Turkey, or from Alexandria in Egypt, or from Cyprus. It was very heavily influenced by Turkish and Arabic music. If you went to a Greek nightclub or coffeehouse in New York or Boston, the music was Greek, but the professional musicians playing it could have been from anywhere. They were Greeks, Turks, Armenians, Egyptians—it didn't matter. Some of those people weren't even supposed to like one another—everyone's heard about how Greeks and Turks don't get along, for example—but when they were playing music together, they got along just fine."

Peter's First Oud, and Many Others

Peter took violin lessons from about the age of ten, and he showed a lot of talent from the start. But unfortunately a muscle problem in his neck soon put an end to his violin playing. "The doctor told me I had to stop, but I kept playing on my own after school," he says with a smile. "But then the neighbors told on me. My mother locked the violin up in a closet, and that was that." At fourteen he began taking mandolin lessons from an old musician who appreciated his talent and gave him lessons for free. But soon Peter decided that what he really wanted to play was the oud.

"At Greek and Armenian parties, I kept hanging out by the bandstand, listening to the oud players and watching their technique. Finally when I was sixteen, I asked a player if he knew where I could

get an oud. Simple, as it turned out. He offered to sell me an extra one of his own." But there was a problem. The price, seventy dollars, was much more than Peter had. "Finally a friend went to him and asked him to reduce the price to fifty dollars. Then my father gave me half of that, and I had just enough of my own to make up the rest." Then there was the matter of getting strings, and an eagle-feather quill to pluck the strings with, which was not so easy. But eventually everything was ready, and he taught himself to play, mainly by listening to his father's records.

A friend bought an oud, too, so they could play together, but this was a really old, beat-up instrument that needed a lot of work. And, of course, the work was done by Peter. Word spread about how well he had done it, and soon Peter was informally in the instrument-repair business even before he finished high school.

Peter showing off the back of
a recently completed oud

Then he went off to college, intending to become an art teacher.

"While I was in college, I got a part-time job in a violin maker's shop," he recalls. Then in one of his courses, he decided to make an oud as a term project. "I think the teacher was a little bit amazed that I was able to turn out a whole, finished stringed instrument. And it played pretty well, too." Peter had found his calling.

Unique Strings

Back home after college, Peter set up his first shop in his mother's basement, making and repairing musical instruments, especially ouds. He soon gained a reputation for work of exceptional quality. He married a young woman from the Armenian community (so now their children have roots in two different immigrant American traditions), and opened his shop in Belmont. He guesses that in the past thirty years, he's made five or six ouds a year on average, maybe a total of 175. "That's not enough to make a living," he said. "My real bread and butter is instrument repairs. I'll fix any kind of stringed instrument. But even that, to me, is creative work. Whenever I repair an instrument, I also look for ways to make it better than it ever was in the first place."

Occasionally someone will bring him a job that stumps him. "I've had a few instruments in here, strange things from Central Asia, that sometimes were really damaged and had parts missing. And if I didn't know the instrument at all, I couldn't even guess what the missing parts should look like. Not very often, but maybe a half dozen times, I've had to just shake my head and say 'sorry, I don't know what to do with that.'"

Making an oud takes expert knowledge and a lot of skill. The soundboard has to be perfectly flat, the neck perfectly straight. The pear-shaped body is made of many separate strips of wood, shaped and planed to fit perfectly and put together on a special wooden block that holds the pieces while the glue dries. Beauty is important, too; in one recent instrument, the body was made of alternating strips of taffy-brown vermilion wood and white-blonde spruce. For every oud he makes, Peter carves a rose-shaped insert that fits into the hole in the soundboard; the design is his alone, a unique signature for his work. Most of Peter's ouds are custom-made for professional musicians, and he admits to a feeling of pride when a new oud is strung and played for the first time. "Nobody has to say anything. What matters is between me, the instrument, and the person playing." When Peter was awarded a National Heritage Fellowship for 2001, it was a much-deserved recognition of his genius.

Will the Tradition Survive?

Peter worries that the Greek American and Armenian American communities are losing their ties to traditional culture. The churches bring people together and serve as the heart of the communities, but the people themselves are often third- or fourth-generation Americans who are losing their old languages and customs. And they no longer live together in Greek or Armenian neighborhoods in cities like Fitchburg. "It's sad to see the old Greek men nowadays," says Peter. "In the old days they would have a coffeehouse or a club where they could get together every day and drink coffee and talk in Greek. Now the coffeehouses are all gone, and the old men sit on benches in the malls looking like lost souls."

The Greek nightclubs of Boston and New York are mostly gone, too, and with them the opportunity for professional musicians to find steady work. And there

The unique rosette design that is Peter's "signature" on an oud

are other signs that traditions are vanishing. "It used to be that the idea of a Greek wedding without Greek dancing was unthinkable," says Peter. "But now they are just as likely to have a deejay as a real band. Maybe at that wedding there would be one child ready to be inspired by a musician playing the oud or some other instrument, a child who would want to go home and learn to play too. How is that child going to be inspired by a deejay?"

What will probably save oud music in America is that the oud is used so widely in the Middle East. There are many recent immigrants to America from Turkey, Palestine, Yemen, and other Middle Eastern lands—and they all play ouds or instruments in the oud family. The music, the languages, the dances will be different, but the instruments will be the same; and the best of the professional musicians will want to buy their custom-made ouds from Peter Kyvelos.

Afterword

For the past ten years I have worked as a deejay. The music I spin includes hip-hop, drum and bass, and other forms of dance music, including Bhangra. Many people have remarked that I am preserving a cultural tradition, and some have even thanked me. I find that ironic. What would my great-grandmother say if she saw me playing music in a nightclub for people dancing and consuming alcohol? Would she feel I was maintaining tradition of some kind?

I feel that what I am doing is acknowledging the positive and enjoyable part of my heritage. My heritage comes not only from Punjab/Pakistan/India, but also from growing up in New York.

Experiencing the birth of hip-hop was as significant a moment in my life as the Bhangra cassette my mom got for me from England when I was a teenager. For me, New York City is a global mecca of cultures colliding. My role as a deejay is to be a conduit in that mix.

Deejaying is a way of communicating by exposing people to a variety of different cultural practices through sound and space. In my work, what I do is as much about creating a space as it is about spinning the music that people dance to. For

"Bhangra" is a percussion-based folk music that originates from Punjab, a region divided by India and Pakistan. Current forms incorporate various dance genres. Bhangra is primarily produced in the United Kingdom.

creating, or rather recreating, the experience of connection to one's place of origin is as much an imagined experience as a likely reality. The place I am "taking them back to" doesn't really exist.

A lot of Bhangra music talks nostalgically about Punjab, the area where the music originated, as a wondrous, fertile land producing bountiful, endless harvests. The reality is that it is a farming state in the Third World. Where I can take them is a place that they and I create, one that combines my musical history and travels and the technology I use to transmit the sounds. Technology makes our world smaller, but also allows us to communicate things in many different ways.

As a British-born second-generation *desi* as well as a native New Yorker, I understand that my influences are as complex and multilayered as those of the people who dance at my parties. What I do is a journey. But I share this journey, for it is my goal to take my audience on one as well. I am the medium—just another traveler, passing on my finds.

DJ Rekha performing at the Smithsonian Folklife Festival's New York City program in 2001

DJ Rekha

Glossary

Aikido (Japanese: "harmonized energy way"). A martial arts technique that emphasizes controlled breathing and a range of holds and throwing maneuvers. See also hapkido.

Alexander the Great (356–323 B.C.). King of Macedonia who conquered an empire extending from Greece to Egypt, Persia, Central Asia, and India.

Baklava. A Middle Eastern dessert made of thin pastry, nuts, and rose-water-flavored syrup.

Bar mitzvah (Hebrew: "what is divinely commanded for a son"). Coming-of-age ceremony for a Jewish boy, usually at age thirteen, and typically celebrated by a feast or party.

Black belt. A belt worn by martial arts students who have advanced beyond the level of basic proficiency. *See also* dan.

Bodhidharma (sixth century A.D.) Semilegendary Indian monk who founded the branch of Buddhism known as Zen. *See also* Zen.

Dalai Lama (Tibetan/Mongolian: "Ocean [of wisdom] monk"). Spiritual leader of Tibetan Buddhism. The present Dalai Lama is the fourteenth holder of the title, each believed to be a reincarnation of the one before.

Dan. The degree or level of proficiency attained by a practitioner of the martial arts, often indicated by the color or type of belt worn.

Desi (pronounced THEY-see; from Hindi *desh*, "country"). Slang term, widely used in South Asian immigrant communities, for a person of Indian, Pakistani, or Bangladeshi ancestry, especially someone now living in the West.

Do, dao ("Way"; Japanese and Korean pronunciation is *do*; Chinese is *dao*). In East Asian philosophy, a set of principles and techniques forming a coherent teaching or doctrine. Schools of martial arts are often called *do* (e.g., aikido, judo).

Doire. A drum made of a hide drumhead stretched on a wooden hoop or frame, widely used in Central Asian music.

Doura. Same as *doire*.

Emir. ("Chieftain" or "prince"). Title used by rulers of some countries in the premodern Islamic world, particularly in Central Asia.

Emirate. A country or state ruled by an emir.

Erhu. A Chinese bowed stringed instrument, with a long neck, small cylindrical body, and two strings.

Ethnic cleansing. The forcible expulsion of ethnic minorities from a certain territory, or their extermination within the territory; the term was widely used during the wars following the breakup of the former country of Yugoslavia in the 1990s.

Eurasia. Term for the single continental land mass north and east of Africa; the division of this continent into "Europe" and "Asia" is a matter of cultural, historic, and ethnic convention rather than geographical fact.

Genghiz Khan (1162–1227). Organizer of a grand confederation of the tribes of Mongolia, and conqueror of much of Asia, from northern China through Central Asia and Persia to the fringes of Eastern Europe. Also spelled Genghis, Jinghiz, Chinggis, etc.

Geshe. A degree given in the Buddhist university system of Tibet and neighboring countries, equivalent to a doctorate in the Western university system.

Gidjak. A long-necked bowed stringed instrument used in Central Asian music.

Green Tara. A Tibetan Buddhist goddess, symbolizing the potentiality of the Buddha for infinite compassion.

Hapkido (Korean: "harmonized energy way"). A school of martial arts that employs techniques borrowed from several other schools, including various holds, throws, and kicks. The word *hapkido* is written with the same Chinese characters as Japanese *aikido*, but the two schools of martial arts are not the same. *See also* aikido.

Jashn-e mehregan. The Persian autumn festival, celebrated in early October. It is a harvest thanksgiving festival; special dishes are made to be given to the poor and needy.

Judo (Japanese: "yielding way"). Martial arts technique emphasizing using an opponent's strength and momentum to one's own advantage; similar to jujitsu but with emphasis on competitive sport rather than actual combat.

Jujitsu (Japanese: "yielding technique"). Martial arts technique emphasizing using an opponent's strength and momentum to one's own advantage; similar to judo but with emphasis on personal combat rather than competitive sport.

Karate (Japanese: "empty hand"; formerly written with characters meaning "Chinese hand," pronounced "tang soo" in Korean). Martial arts technique emphasizing powerful punches and chops made with the bare hand.

Kendo (Japanese: "sword way"). Japanese-style fencing, using wooden or bamboo swords.

Khan (Turkish and Mongolian: "chieftain"). Leader of a tribe or confederation of tribes, among the nomadic peoples of Central Asia.

Ki (Pronounced "ch'i" or "qi" in Chinese, "ki" in Korean and Japanese). A type of energy believed in East Asian medicine and philosophy to circulate within the body; martial arts techniques aim to concentrate and focus *ki* to increase one's fighting ability.

Klezmer. Jewish folk music of Eastern Europe, often strongly influenced by Middle Eastern and Gypsy music.

Kubilai Khan (1216–1294). A grandson of Genghiz Khan who led the Mongol conquest of China and founded China's Yuan Dynasty of Mongol rulers (1279–1368).

Kung fu (Chinese: "skill"). A martial arts technique emphasizing using hands and feet to strike numerous blows in succession.

Lute. Stringed musical instrument with a neck of variable length and a pear-shaped body; a European version of the oud. The lute family includes all stringed instruments generally similar to lutes and ouds. *See also* oud.

Mandala (Sanskrit: "circle"). A picture or diagram, usually of squares within circles, used in Buddhism and other Asian religions as a symbol of the universe.

Mandolin. A European stringed instrument in the lute family, similar in shape to a lute but considerably smaller.

Mao Zedong (1893–1976; formerly spelled Mao Tse-tung). Leader of the Chinese Communist revolution of 1949 and head of the government of the People's Republic of China, 1949–1976.

Martial arts. Techniques of personal combat, usually involving intensive training, a philosophical outlook, and an organized system of competition and ranking according to skill.

Meditation. A process of intense mental concentration, leaving the mind tranquil, harmonious, free of distractions, and able to focus without conscious thought or direction.

Mortar and pestle. A deep, cylindrical container (mortar) and a rod-shaped pounding instrument (pestle), used to pulverize and mix ingredients for cooking.

Nan. Flatbread found in many varieties all around the Middle East, Central Asia, and South Asia.

Nomad. A person with no permanent place of residence, who travels from place to place according to the availability of employment, food, water. *See also* pastoral nomad.

Nowruz. The Persian New Year festival, held on the first day of spring and widely celebrated throughout Central Asia. It is the most important holiday of the Persian year, marked by prolonged feasting with special foods.

Nush-e Jan (Persian: "bon appétit"). Polite Persian phrase inviting a person to eat and enjoy something.

Oud (Arabic *al'ūd*: "twig," "wood"). A stringed musical instrument having a medium-length neck, multiple strings, and a pear-shaped body, widely used in various Eastern Mediterranean cultures. *See also* lute.

Pastoral nomad. Member of a tribe or people living by raising livestock and traveling seasonally from place to place according to the availability of pasture and water.

Pilaf. A dish made by mixing cooked rice with meat, vegetables, and other ingredients, or by baking rice and other ingredients together.

Pinyin (Chinese: "combined sounds"). A system for spelling the sounds of Chinese words using the Roman alphabet.

Qu (Chinese: "song," "musical drama"). Chinese opera, a theatrical form combining instrumental music, singing, drama, spoken dialogue, mime, and other dramatic techniques. *See also* xi.

Revolutionary opera. A type of Chinese opera created in the 1960s, emphasizing themes of Communist revolution and intended to replace traditional opera.

Samovar. A large kettle, usually with a built-in coal- or charcoal-burning heater, used to keep hot water or tea hot and ready to serve.

Samurai (Japanese: "servant"). A traditional Japanese warrior, bound by vows of loyalty to a master and expected to be expert in various types of martial arts, both armed and unarmed.

Setar. Small, four-stringed instrument played similarly to the guitar or banjo.

Shab-e yalda. Persian winter feast, held on the night of the winter solstice (late December), with bonfires and dishes of fruit to symbolize the return of light after the winter darkness.

Shaolin. Name of a Chinese Buddhist temple in Henan Province, known as a center for traditional martial arts training.

Shashmaqam (Persian: "music in six forms"). The distinctive traditional music of Central Asia, now associated especially with the Bukharan Jewish community.

Sona. Chinese double-reed wind instrument, similar to an oboe.

Taekwondo (Korean: "trample fist way"). A very vigorous and dangerous form of karate, characterized by powerful kicks and blows with the hand. *See also* karate.

Tanbur. A Central Asian stringed instrument in the lute family, related to the *tar*, with a long neck and a small body.

Tar. A Central Asian stringed instrument in the lute family, related to the *tanbur*, with a long neck and a small body. Along with the *doire* frame-drum, the *tar* is the most basic instrument in Bukharan music.

Timur Leng (1369–1405; also spelled Tamerlane). Turkish-Mongolian conqueror who created an empire in Central Asia, with its capital at Samarkand.

Tribe. A social group based on kinship, language, economic interests, and other criteria, in which the family is the basic social unit and leadership is exercised by consent of the people as a whole.

Wushu (Chinese: "martial arts"). Martial arts in general; also a particular competitive form of martial arts, combining features of several other systems of armed and unarmed combat.

Xi (Chinese: "musical drama"). Chinese opera, a theatrical form combining instrumental music, singing, drama, spoken dialogue, mime, and other dramatic techniques. *See also* qu.

Yurt (Turkish *yurt* = Mongolian *ger*; "felt tent"). A type of tent used by the pastoral nomads of Central Asia, in which sheets of felt are stretched over a flexible wooden framework, forming the walls and roof.

Zen (Japanese *zen* = Chinese *chan*: "meditation"). A type of Buddhism characterized by emphasis on meditation and self-discipline, often associated with the practice of martial arts.

Suggestions for Further Reading

The Silk Road: General Works, History

Meyer, Karl E., and Shareen Blair Brysac. *Tournament of Shadows: The Great Game and the Race for Empire in Central Asia.* New York: Counterpoint Press, 2000. A history of the complex struggle between Russia and Great Britain for domination of Central Asia in the nineteenth century.

The Silk Road Project, Inc., and the Asia Society. *Silk Road Encounters.* New York: Silk Road Project, Inc., and the Asia Society, 2001. Includes *Sourcebook* (text by John S. Major) and *Teachers Guide* containing lesson plans, resource list, etc.

Travelers on the Silk Road

Larner, John. *Marco Polo and the Discovery of the World.* New Haven: Yale University Press, 1999 (paperback, 2001). A thoughtful study of why Marco Polo's famous *Travels* was so influential in early Renaissance Europe.

Latham Ronald, ed. *The Travels of Marco Polo.* New York: Viking Press, 1982. A fine edition of Marco Polo's classic travel book.

Rossabi, Morris. *Voyager from Xanadu: Rabban Sauma and the First Journey from China to the West.* Tokyo: Kodansha International, 1992. The remarkable story of a Turko-Chinese Christian who traveled to Persia, Baghdad, Rome, and Paris in the thirteenth century as an envoy from Kubilai Khan.

Wriggins, Sally Hovey. *Xuanzang: A Buddhist Pilgrim on the Silk Road.* Boulder, CO: Westview Press, 1998. About an eighth-century Chinese monk who went to India in search of authentic editions of the Buddhist scriptures, an adventure-packed trip that inspired the classic Chinese novel *Journey to the West.*

For Younger Readers

Major, John S., and Stephen Fieser. *The Silk Route: 7,000 Miles of History.* New York: HarperCollins Children's Books, 1995 (HarperTrophy paperback, 1996). A picture book (ages 9–12) that gives a vivid sense of travel and trade along the Silk Road.

"The Silk Road." *Calliope* magazine, February 2002. An entire issue devoted to the Silk Road cultures. A teachers' guide is available on-line. For ages 9 to 14.

Whitfield, Susan, *Life along the Silk Road.* Berkeley: University of California Press (paperback edition), 2001. A highly readable book that uses a number of tenth-century Silk Road travelers (fictional composites) to give a wonderful sense of time and place.

Art and Ideas along the Silk Road

Foltz, Richard C. *Religions of the Silk Road: Overland Trade and Cultural Exchange from Antiquity to the Fifteenth Century.* New York: St. Martin's, 1999. An excellent survey of Silk Road cultural exchange, with emphasis on religions.

Irwin, Robert. *Islamic Art in Context: Art, Architecture, and the Literary World.* New York: Harry N. Abrams, 1997. A topical approach to Islamic art, emphasizing the close ties between art and literature.

Juliano, Annette L., and Judith A. Lerner. *Monks and Merchants: Silk Road Treasures from Northwest China.* New York: Harry N. Abrams with the Asia Society, 2001. A major survey of Silk Road arts found in Northwestern China, lavishly illustrated and with numerous excellent essays on special topics.

Munzo, Jean Paul. Photographs by Ferdinand Kouziomov. *Central Asian Art.* New York: Parkstone Press, 1997. Pays particular attention to Central Asian architecture and architectural ornament; spectacular photographs.

Rhie, Marylin M., and Robert A. F. Thurman. Photographs by John Bigelow Taylor. *Wisdom and Compassion: The Sacred Art of Tibet.* New York: Arbradale Press (expanded edition), 2000. The definitive book on Tibetan sacred art, beautifully illustrated and with clear and intelligent text.

Music

Levin, Theodore. *The Hundred Thousand Fools of God: Musical Travels in Central Asia (and Queens, New York).* Bloomington: Indiana University Press, 1996. The author's encounters with musicians in several parts of Central Asia and in the Bukharan Jewish community in Queens, New York; includes a CD.

Ma, Yo-Yo, and Elizabeth ten Grotenhuis. *Along the Silk Road.* Seattle: University of Washington Press, 2002. The renowned cellist describes his musical adventures in Asia and his ongoing Silk Road Project; essays by several contributors on the arts and cultures of the Silk Road, with emphasis on music.

MacKerras, Colin. *Peking Opera.* Oxford: Oxford University Press, 1997. A concise, clear, attractively illustrated introduction to Peking Opera, part of Oxford's Images of Asia series.

For Younger Readers

Shepard, Aaron. Illustrated by Song Nan Zhang. *Lady White Snake: A Tale from Chinese Opera.* Union City, CA: Pan Asian Publications, 2001. A nicely illustrated retelling (for ages 7–11) of the classic Chinese opera tale, with useful supplementary material about Chinese opera, acting, and costumes.

Paper and Writing

Bloom, Jonathan. *Paper before Print: The History and Impact of Paper in the Islamic World.* New Haven: Yale University Press, 2001. Paper, invented in China around 100 B.C., was being produced in quantity in eighth-century Samarkand and eventually made its way via the Islamic world to Europe. A fascinating tale of cultural and technological exchange along the Silk Road.

Lindqvist, Cecelia. *China: Empire of Living Symbols.* New York: Addison-Wesley, 1989. A wonderful introduction to the Chinese written language in its cultural context, with step-by-step instructions for writing many characters.

Mathews, Thomas F., and Roger S. Wieck, eds. *Treasures in Heaven: Armenian Illuminated Manuscripts.* New York: Pierpont Morgan Library, 1994. Sumptuously illustrated catalogue of an exhibition of rare Armenian illuminated manuscripts.

Robinson, Andrew. *The Story of Writing.* London: Thames & Hudson, 1995. Chapters on the major scripts of the world, with emphasis on ancient writing systems and how they were discovered and deciphered.

For Younger Readers

Halliday, Peter. *Creative Calligraphy.* New York: Larousse Kingfisher Chambers, 1995. A very good introduction to the art and craft of calligraphy.

Food and Cooking

Batmanglij, Najmieh Khalili. *New Food of Life: Ancient Persian and Modern Iranian Cooking and Ceremonies*. Washington: Mage Publications, 1992. Excellent recipes and a wonderful account of the social settings of food in Persian/Iranian culture.

Batmanglij, Najmieh Khalili. *Silk Road Cooking: A Vegetarian Journey*. Washington: Mage Publications, 2002. Central Asian vegetarian cooking; a friendly cookbook well suited to younger readers.

For Younger Readers

Cook, Deanna F. *The Kids' Multicultural Cookbook*. Charlotte, VT: Williamson Publishers, 1995. Features tasty and easy-to-make dishes from around the world, including the Middle East and East Asia.

Martial Arts

Morgan, Forrest E. *Living the Martial Way: A Manual for the Way a Modern Warrior Should Think*. Fort Lee, NJ: Barricade Books, 1992. One of the best overall guides to the martial arts as sport, self-defense, and way of life.

Saltzman, Mark. *Iron and Silk*. New York: Random House, 1986 (Vintage Departures paperback, 1987). A young Yale graduate discovers the martial arts and the philosophy behind them during a year in China.

For Younger Readers

Devens, Richard, and Norman Sandler. *Martial Arts for Kids: The Road to Inner Strength, Self-Awareness, and a Peaceful World*. Tokyo: Weatherhill, 1997. A nice introduction for upper-elementary through early high-school children to the marital arts and the philosophy they embody.

Rugs

Gregorian, John B. *Oriental Rugs of the Silk Route: Culture, Process, and Selection*. New York: Rizzoli International, 2000. A good general introduction to rugs from various Silk Road cultures.

Scott, Gordon W. *An Illustrated Guide to Making Oriental Rugs*. Florence, OR: Pacific Search Press, 1984. A very detailed guide to setting up a loom, various kinds of rug knots, and other essential techniques for Oriental rug weaving. Very helpful in understanding how rugs are made and how much labor goes into each one.

Index